The Valerons - No Boundaries!

Some men operate beyond the law's reach. Such are the Macreedys. They sell whiskey to the Indians across the Canadian border, then cash in their loot (including the ill-gotten gain from the selling of Indian women and children) and return to their horse ranch outside of Rimrock, Wyoming, outwardly living respectable lives.

But the killing of an ex-Mountie in Wyoming reveals their fiendish operation to three travelers. Unfortunately for the Macreedys, one of those travelers is Scarlet Valeron, who promises the dying MP that her family will see justice done. However, without proof of a crime, the local law enforcers can do nothing, so it is left to the Valerons to figure a plan that will expose the Macreedys for the criminals they are. If that fails – well, a Valeron has made a promise – Justice will be served!

By the same author

Dead Man's Canyon
Garrett's Trail to Justice
High Bounty at Wayward
Hard Trail to Breadneck Pass
Valeron's Range
The Valeron Code
Valeron's Justice

The Valerons - No Boundaries!

Terrell L. Bowers

ROBERT HALE

First published in Great Britain 2017

ISBN 978-0-7198-2501-9

The Crowood Press
The Stable Block
Crowood Lane
Ramsbury
Marlborough
Wiltshire SN8 2HR

www.bhwesterns.com

Robert Hale is an imprint
of The Crowood Press

Typeset by
Derek Doyle & Associates, Shaw Heath
Printed and bound in Great Britain by
CPI Group (UK) Ltd, Croydon, CR0 4YY

CHAPTER ONE

Although the North West Mounted Police did what they could, whiskey traders continued to slip across the US border and sell their firewater to the various Indian tribes. The worst of these traded not only for horses, animal pelts, buffalo robes, and anything gold or silver; they even took the wives and children who were offered up by some of the more desperate drink-dependent Indians.

Constables Brock Gordon, his younger brother, John, and a third Mountie named Young were dispatched when they learned one of the whiskey traders was taking women and children in trade for booze.

Many of Sitting Bull's tribe had crossed back over the border to surrender to the US Army, but there was still a sizable number of Sioux, Blackfeet, Crees and Bloods with whom to deal.

'Their camp is twenty miles or so from Fort Walsh,' the half-breed guide, known only as Skeet, told them. 'One of the Sioux told me it was the same bunch he traded his eldest daughter to last time. I believe they have a couple more Indian children now, plus Big Nose traded his wife to them.'

'Despicable scoundrels, these liquor dealers,' Brock said. 'Running them off is not enough, especially this bunch – they are selling those poor Indians into a life of slavery . . . or worse. I say we capture and arrest these dirty maggots.'

'Sounds good, big brother,' John agreed. 'Make an example of a few and word might reach the rest of the whiskey-dealing vermin.'

'I'm with you,' Constable Young put in. 'Let's see to it they lose everything they have gained. We can dump the barrels of whiskey and confiscate their wagons and horses. If they do manage to escape, they will return to America with nothing but the clothes on their backs!'

It was summer so they weren't burdened down with extra clothing and the horses moved easily over the terrain. They continued until they were nearing the area where the whiskey dealers had set up camp.

'There's a clearing near the creek, another half-mile or so,' Skeet informed them. 'I got close enough to see the smoke from their camp.'

'We can take them from two different sides, so they don't make a fight of it,' Young outlined – he, being the senior MP of the three, took charge. 'Me and John will go in from the west side. You two swing around and come in from the east. We can swoop in and have them trapped between us.'

'How do we manage to arrive at the same time?' Brock asked.

Young removed his pocket watch. 'Let's figure thirty minutes – then we go.'

'Should be ample time,' Skeet said. 'We'll circle behind the hills until we get downwind of the camp. Then we'll come in with guns at the ready.'

With the plan in place, Brock and the guide began to move through the trees. This was not going to be Brock's first time dealing with whiskey traders, but they didn't always try to capture them. It was usually enough that, when the lowlife mongrels spotted a Mountie, they left much of their cargo behind and beat a hasty retreat across the border. In Brock's four different encounters, there had only been one shot fired – and it had been a whiskey dealer warning his comrades. Most whiskey traders wanted to avoid a shootout with the Mounted Police. They were gaining a reputation for running down desperadoes who crossed certain lines.

The two men were almost to the point of turning in the direction of the outlaw camp when a dozen Indians suddenly appeared on the trail ahead – all of them brandishing weapons! Skeet and Brock hurried to cut them off.

The warriors showed an immediate respect for the scarlet-coated trooper with the high boots and odd helmet. They stopped as Skeet and the Mountie reined up before them.

Skeet had a gift for a mix of language and sign, able to converse with all of the tribes. He asked where they were going, armed for war.

After a short exchange, he shook his head and explained the situation to Brock. 'Some of the whiskey Big Nose traded his wife for yesterday was tainted. Big Nose fell off his horse and spilled much of his liquor, plus a couple of the Indians have died and another two are blind. They are on their way to punish the traders.'

'Tell them we will handle this,' Brock instructed. 'If they kill those men, it might start a war with the Americans.'

'I told them we. . . .'

But the sound of gunfire suddenly erupted. Not one or two shots, but a dozen or more rang out. Alarm flashed on Skeet's face and he jerked his horse around.

'Those aren't MP guns doing the shooting!' he cried. 'John and Young are under attack!'

Brock didn't wish to involve the Indians, but as he turned his mount and dug in his heels, the warriors followed along. If they ended up in a fight, at least they and the braves would be on the same side.

It turned out the camp was more difficult to reach than anticipated. It took Skeet almost five minutes to reach the place and they arrived too late to help. Two wagons and a tent were still in place, but all of the horses were gone, along with the loot and whatever Indian females or children that had been traded for the vile hard liquor. All that remained were a couple barrels of whiskey and some supplies.

Brock took all of that in with a single sweep of the encampment, but it was the three bodies that drew his attention. John and Young must have been spotted, as their bodies lay some distance from the fire-pits. Another body was on the ground. It was one of the whiskey traders who had not escaped the gunfight. He was writhing in pain, gut-shot, and sure to die.

Skeet checked on Young, while Brock hurried to his

brother's body. The Indians forgot about revenge, suddenly interested only in grabbing the whiskey and supplies. Even Big Nose had no concern for the loss of his wife. The damnable liquor was all he could think of – even if it turned out to be half-poison like the last batch he and his people had drank.

Brock gently lifted John's lifeless body enough to cradle him in his arms. It was Brock who had insisted they join the Mounted Police. He had been the one looking for adventure and excitement. John had followed his big brother since he was a child and had come along for his sake. Now this great adventure had cost John his life.

Skeet moved from the fallen Young to see to the wounded trader. He offered him some of his own whiskey for the pain, asking him questions about his comrades.

Within minutes, the Indians had taken everything of value and left the camp. John finally lowered his brother's body to the ground and went over to stand over Skeet and the dying whiskey-trader. The urge to shoot him was strong, but the man was suffering so much pain, it would have been doing him a favor.

'There were six others in the group,' Skeet told Brock. 'They have a place several hundred miles away on the other side of the border.'

'America is a big place,' Brock said. 'We need more than that.'

Skeet gave him a hard stare. 'What does it matter?' he asked. 'The NWMP can't cross the border. All you can do is inform the authorities in Montana and hope they are able to arrest the killers.'

Brock snorted his contempt. 'A lot of good that will do.

There are no witnesses to the ambush and no one is going to accept the word of a drunk-out-of-his-head Indian like Big Nose.'

'They will have the Indians they took with them.'

'You and I both know they will sell them to the first buyer they can find.'

'Brock,' Skeet said gravely, 'I know how much your brother meant to you, but you have to let this go. You can make a report and hope the Americans catch these men. It's all you can do.'

'What about you and me going after them?'

Skeet lowered his eyes. 'When I cross the border again I'm going to be like a gust of wind – here or there and gone. There are warrants out for my arrest from when I was buying guns for the Indians. I'm sorry, but that's how it is.'

'I understand,' Brock said.

'Tell you what I will do,' Skeet offered. 'I'll stick with the wounded man until he dies, then bury his body. You go ahead and take John and Young back to the post. It will save you a little time.'

'Thanks, Skeet. I want to get after those men as quickly as possible.'

Reese Valeron was the eldest of the three families of Valeron children. His father, Locke, had taught him how to manage and oversee the massive ranch. It was something Reese enjoyed, a fine life for a man with the energy and intellect to handle several chores at once. He was also good with people, and had learned that designating duties and responsibilities to several reliable men was much easier than trying to do everything himself.

The one thing Reese didn't have much time for was fun or the traveling most of his family and cousins enjoyed. Regardless, when Landau told him of Locke's idea, he was at first reluctant.

'Come on,' Landau coaxed. 'You haven't been off of the ranch since we all were in Brimstone together. You didn't even make it to Nash's wedding. Everyone needs to get away from their work once in a while.'

'I don't know,' Reese contended. 'Anyone can check out the new machinery and gear we ordered.'

'It's a chance for you to pay your respects to Nash and his new wife, then spend a couple days in Denver,' Landau continued his appeal. 'You know Scarlet has been looking forward to this trip for weeks.'

An enlightened glint came into Reese's eyes. 'Yeah, and you don't figure my folks favor you going alone as her chaperon. I know when I'm being used – you think I'll be more . . . accommodating than Jared.'

'Well, your mother does stand firmly on propriety. It's one thing for me to take Scarlet to town for supplies, but quite another to accompany her on an extended trip like this.'

Reese gave the man an intense look. 'This is it for you, isn't it? I mean, you are looking to propose?'

'Denver would be the perfect place,' Landau didn't deny his intentions. 'There are some nice restaurants to choose from.' Landau gave a one-shoulder shrug. 'You know my past, Reese. I reckon you know about my mistakes too.'

'Scarlet had to confide your life's story to Jared . . .

when he insisted we hang you for your part in her kidnapping. And Jared . . . well, he keeps secrets about as good as he holds his temper.'

Landau laughed. 'That brother of yours – never met an outlaw he didn't want to hang.'

'The thing is, Brett made sure your name was cleared before he took over as the Valeron town marshal. There was never any formal charge made against you for the man you killed. He was a well-known womanizer. In fact, more than a few of the married men who lived nearby were thrilled when he ended up dead.'

'It doesn't excuse my riding with a gang for several months. I mean, I never hurt anyone personally, but I tended the horses and helped with the getaways.'

'The family understands about your situation, but you've proved yourself worthy by siding us time and again.'

'I'm still not good enough for your sister.'

Reese laughed. 'My sister will get the man she wants . . . and if you're the man, so be it. You've got the courage and dedication to be in charge of a good portion of this ranch. And with Brett and Nash no longer living on the place, there's room for another son . . .' grinning, '. . . or a son-in-law to help out.'

'Then you'll go with us?'

'Have you spoken to Pa?' Reese wanted to know. 'I mean, Scarlet is old enough to give her consent with or without him, but you know she will want his blessing.'

'Yeah, I manned up and told him this idea of mine some time ago. He gave me the go-ahead, but said I had to stay within the bounds of acceptable conduct to please your mother. I'm certain she will approve of this arrangement – providing you accompany us.'

'All right. I'll tell Sketcher to oversee the place for a few days. He has been complaining that I never let him run things.'

Landau chuckled. 'Yeah, plus, he's run out of people to sketch.'

'He's real handy with that pencil. Did you see the drawing he did of Tish and Nessy?'

'Cliff gave him five dollars for it,' Landau replied. 'Bought a frame for it and all. He put it on the wall in Nessy's room.'

'Well, the one he did of me made me look like an old man,' Reese complained.

'He has the eye of an artist,' Landau teased. 'All work and no play makes you look like an old man before your time. That's why you need to take this trip with me and Scarlet. You could use a little downtime from working the ranch seven days a week.'

'You can stop spreading frosting on the cake, Landau. I said I'll go.'

'Thanks, Reese,' the hired man said. 'Thanks a lot.'

Stewart Macreedy grunted his satisfaction at receiving the small sack of gold dust. He waved to Eddie to bring the two Indian girls – aged about nine to eleven years of age – over to the man who had paid for them.

Washta hugged each one, desperately wishing she could do something to save them. Both of the small-framed waifs clung to her tightly. The tears wet their cheeks and they cried at being taken from her care. She had served as their temporary mother and protector. But now – now they were being sold into slavery. Mere children, they would never see their people again.

Eddie gave them only a moment with Washta, then dragged them by the arms and led them away. They were tight-lipped and no longer crying by the time they were pushed towards the strange man. Being female Indian children, they did not fight against their new master. They had been raised to accept whatever life threw at them, regardless of the rigors and degradation. Once loaded into an enclosed carriage, Washta watched them start down the road. She regained her composure, left on her own with the whiskey dealers.

'What about Washta?' Quinn asked Stewart. 'She's a sight prettier than any Indian squaw I ever seen. Bet we can get a fair price for her.'

'She's got white blood in her,' Stewart guessed. 'I'm pretty sure she understands English too. Might even speak it.'

'Captive, you think?'

'Could be. I asked her some questions, but she plays dumb. From the old bruises she's packing, Big Nose was not gentle with his captive squaw.'

'Wonder if they had any kids?'

'Big Nose said no. I asked when he brought her to trade. Of course, that doesn't mean the two of them didn't have a nit or two that died from the cold or something. Makes no difference any more; she belongs to us.'

'Remember the French trapper from over Powder River way? He said he'd pay good money for a pretty little squaw.'

'I've a notion to keep Washta for ourselves,' Stewart told his younger brother. 'We need someone to do the cooking and cleaning around the place. That last hired cook was a lousy housekeeper and couldn't boil water without burning it.'

'She was Mexican,' Quinn reminded him. 'If we were of a mind to eat nothing but peppers, beans and tortillas, we might have thought she was a better cook.'

'I'll be glad when we're home. These trips take forever, and this one cost us the loss of our wagons and supplies. By the time we replace everything, we won't be able to pay the mortgage. It was due two months ago, and I promised the banker we'd get him his money.'

'I doubt the banker will try and sell it out from under us. After all, we did pay up the back taxes on the place.'

'Maybe,' Stewart said. 'But losing our wagon and supplies is not going to help. I'll see if we have enough left to pay something to the bank, after we get our next shipment ready to go.'

'Gonna be risky going back so soon, especially after killing those two Mounties, Stu.'

'You know Eddie,' Stewart excused their youngest brother. 'He got spooked and started shooting. Once Korkle and Frost joined in. . . .' He didn't have to finish. 'We'll hope everything has calmed down by the time we cross back up that way again.'

'Real shame about Frost. Them Mounties were pretty good shots.'

'He was still alive when we left him,' Stewart reminded him. 'If someone got him to talk, it could be real trouble.'

'Them MPs would have caught us cold, if Seevy hadn't

warned us the Indians were coming, looking to take our scalps. I told you there was something wrong with that one barrel of whiskey. It just didn't taste or look right.'

'Yes, but we could have dealt with the Indians. A little free liquor would have made them happy. If those Mounties hadn't shown up. . . .' Stewart swore. 'Well, it's too late to change anything. They seldom have more than a couple in any one area. Unless this was a special raid, we killed the only law for miles around. No one will know who it was – might even blame Big Nose.'

'Unless Frost talked.'

'The Indians wouldn't bother questioning him, and he was done for. I doubt he survived for more than a couple hours. No, Big Nose and his bunch will have been hell-bent to grab the two barrels of booze and supplies we left behind. I reckon Frost died without anyone giving him a second look.'

Quinn sighed, resigned to worry. 'All the same, Seevy is gonna keep an eye on our back-trail. He said we should make the circle he suggested, in case someone does try to follow after us.'

'Yeah, yeah,' his older brother grumbled. 'It's a waste of time and an extra week on the trail, but we'll play the game by his rules. I just want to get back to Rimrock and pretend to be struggling horse ranchers again. We'll get a new wagon to replace the one we lost, then start brewing for the next trip.'

'You're the boss, Stu,' Quinn told him. 'Where you lead, me and Eddie follow.'

'Tell everyone to keep their paws off the Injun gal. If we treat her decent, she might settle in and do us a good job of being our cook and housekeeper. Don't want her getting her hackles up and trying to poison us or something.'

'Right. I'll tell the others – especially Noonan – to keep their hands off of the squaw.'

Brock could not shake the depression, but he doggedly kept on the trail. The whiskey traders had taken Young and John's horses along with their own. Two days had passed before he was able to set out after the murderers. It had been a difficult decision, resigning from the NWMP, but he could not forget or forgive the murder of his little brother.

There was quite a lot of activity near the Canada/United States border, as many of the Sioux were being forced to return to the States. Sitting Bull and five thousand Indians had taken refuge in Canada after the battle at a place called The Little Big Horn. Pursued by a relentless army, seeking retribution for the deaths of nearly two hundred soldiers, the Sioux had taken up residence north of the US border for the past several years. But the buffalo herds had diminished and the Canadian government could no longer feed such a large contingent of immigrants. They finally cut off supplies and, facing starvation, many of the Sioux began to cross the border and surrender to US authorities. They were then escorted to the reservations that had been set aside for them. With groups that mounted into the hundreds moving from Canada to the US, tracking a small, singular bunch of horses was not an option.

Brock was forced to check at trading posts and talk to

anyone he came into contact with. It took almost a week before he met someone who had bought a couple horses from several white men, who were traveling with two Indian girls, a squaw and four draft animals. From that point, he ascertained their direction and set after them. To ensure he remained on their trail, he painstakingly stopped at each settlement or post along the way so he did not lose them.

Days accumulated and his money dwindled to almost nothing. He sold off his brother's possessions and most of his own. He was soon down to a few dollars and eating mostly beans, jerky and hard rolls. But the life of a Mountie offered few frills and a man stayed lean and tough. He was used to hardship and getting by on the barest of necessities. Brock pushed on, constantly mindful of the needs of his horse, forced to rest and allow the animal feed whenever it was available.

Finally, after he had crossed all of Montana, he ventured endless miles over wide open country and discovered he was in Wyoming. His tenacity eventually paid dividends. Soon he was on the very tracks of the six men for whom he had been searching. He knew it was them, because a couple hunters had seen the group and wondered about them traveling with an Indian squaw. From the description, it was Big Nose's woman.

Tired, aching, constantly suffering from hunger and lack of sleep, Brock grew impatient. He began to increase the speed of his jaded mount. Within the back of his mind, he wondered how he would capture and transport so many men back to Canada all by himself. But nothing was going to impede his quest. He was close now. Soon, he would catch a glimpse of them, riding placidly along, without a concern in the world, satisfied they were safely in their homeland.

'It's a noose or prison cell for the remainder of your years,' Brock grumbled aloud. 'And if you put up a fight, I'll settle the score without taking. . . .'

Something hit him hard in the chest. As the sudden stab of pain went through him, the sound of a gunshot echoed in his ears.

Brock folded forward, attempting to cling to the saddle. But his horse spooked at the unexpected gunblast. It danced sideways and Brock – his entire body having gone lax – could not stay aboard. He landed on the ground, lying on his side, with not even the strength to try and get his gun free. He rolled his head to get his face out of the dirt and saw the moccasin boots of the man who had ambushed him.

'Hot damn,' a voice drawled. 'Who'd ever thunk you could track us this fer? Got tuh have the nose of a hound dog, Mountie.'

A toe pushed against his shoulder, rolling Brock onto his back. Through a haze of pain and only barely conscious, he could see the man standing over him. It was a blurry figure, clad in buckskin, with a wide-rimmed floppy hat shading a dirty, bewhiskered face.

'Sorry about them other two Mounties,' the man said. 'Young Eddie got scar't and started shootin'. Weren't nothin' we could do but finish the job.'

Brock tried to muster forth a word, but it lodged in his throat.

'Fool stunt,' the man spoke again. 'You comin' alone

tuh try and take us all by your lonesome. Real gutsy, I'll grant you . . . but don't show fer much betwixt your ears.'

'Y-you killed my brother,' Brock finally managed a few words.

The shooter displayed regret. 'Just bad timin', friend.' He gazed down at Brock, gun poised to fire, but he didn't pull the trigger. 'You're done fer,' he said gravely. 'I'll leave you breathin', so you can clear your conscience with the Man upstairs.'

Brock could not keep his eyes open. He let go to a black void, knowing he had failed his brother yet again.

CHAPTER TWO

Reese preferred horseback, while Scarlet enjoyed the protection of a covered buggy. Landau drove the chaise, which he often used to take Scarlet into Valeron for weekly supplies. It was lightweight, yet durable and comfortable enough to handle a longer trip. The horse was a stocky mare, the same one they used for most of their short jaunts to Valeron.

Their first stop would be Castle Point and an overnight visit with Doctor Nash Valeron and his bride, Trina, who also handled the nursing of patients. After that, they would travel to Cheyenne, leave the animal and rig at the livery and proceed by train to Denver. Two or three nights in the city – making sure that Landau found a time and place for his proposal, and they would return to Cheyenne and then home again.

Reese picked up the trail Jared had told him about; a shortcut to Castle Point that would save several miles. He had led the way along the narrow pathway for a mile or so when he heard the sound of a distant shot. Swinging around to Landau and Scarlet, he was immediately concerned.

'Rifle fire!' he declared. Then looking at the rolling-hill terrain, 'Not much chance of big game out here in the open, except for possibly antelope. I'd best check it out.'

'We'll keep to the trail,' Landau said. 'If you run into trouble, fire off a couple shots.'

Reese acknowledged the plan and put his horse into an easy lope. He didn't want to pop up over the crest of a hill and become a target, so he slowed his mount after a quarter mile. Proceeding with caution, he had only a vague idea of the direction he needed to take. That attentiveness paid off when he spotted a riderless horse. The reins were dangling to the ground and the animal was busy feeding on the sparse grass.

Easing his rifle free of its scabbard, he jacked a shell into the chamber and continued towards the horse. There was a faint outline of an old trail, where a wagon or two had once traveled. The fresh readable sign was that of several horses. However, the nearby hills prevented him from seeing who or how many men had passed by recently.

The horse had an odd-looking saddle and there were bulging saddle-bags and a thick bedroll behind the saddle. He was almost to the grazing mare when he spotted a body a short distance away. Taking another quick look, he saw no one else in sight, so he hurried over to check on the man.

Reese thought the fellow dead, until he gently opened his jacket to check his wound. The move brought forth a weak groan. By the time he had put his own coat under the man's head and given him a sip of water, Scarlet and

Landau arrived.

'We've got some medical supplies under the wagon seat,' Scarlet offered.

Reese shook his head. 'He hasn't got long. I'm surprised he is still breathing. Whoever shot him, hit him dead center.'

Landau joined him and they did what they could to make the man comfortable. Scarlet demonstrated a natural compassion, sitting at his side and taking hold of his hand. After a few moments, the man garnered enough strength to speak. Haltingly, pausing each time the breath left his lungs, he confided his story to the three of them.

'A Mountie?' Scarlet spoke up, once he had forced out the last of his tale. 'All the way down here in Wyoming?'

'Blood runs deep in some families,' Landau said. 'You of all people should know about that, Miss Scarlet.'

'Trouble is, they will get away with the murder of his brother and those Indians,' Reese concluded. 'Wyoming law won't be concerned – probably won't even learn of the crime these men committed in another country.'

'Well, the law can be concerned about Brock Gordon!' Scarlet declared. 'He has been shot and left for dead right here in Wyoming!'

Reese looked off in the direction the killers had gone.

'I'm not the tracker Jared is, but I can see there has been a half-dozen or more horses along here. Some of the tracks appear to be from draft animals.'

'Sounds right,' Landau said. 'He claimed to be after six men and a hostage, and they left their wagon behind. One of those men was alert enough to watch their back trail and he bushwhacked him.'

Scarlet had been listening to them, but a slight pressure to her hand caused her to look back at the Mountie. He gnashed his teeth in pain, but tugged slightly, drawing her closer. She put her ear down next to the man's mouth so she could hear his deathly whisper.

'C-can't die without . . . . My brother. . . .' His voice was raspy, having to force every word to surface with the last of his strength.

'Constable Brock Gordon, North West Mounted Police,' she addressed him sedately, blinking back her tears. 'I give you my word as a Valeron, you have not died in vain. My family will bring the whiskey dealers and the man who shot you to justice. They will pay for what they did in Canada, and for what they did here today. You have my solemn promise.'

The ex-Mountie forced the semblance of a smile to his lips. 'Thank. . . .' But he was unable to manage another word. A breath of air escaped through his lips and his features went lax. Brock Gordon had succumbed to his fate.

'I'll send off a wire when we reach Castle Point,' Reese was the first of the trio to speak. 'Jared can meet me back here – hopefully by tomorrow afternoon – and we'll track these guys down.'

'Miss Scarlet can visit Nash an extra day or two, and I'll join you,' Landau volunteered. 'I intend to see the promise she made is kept.'

Stewart Macreedy rode in silence, as Seevy made his report. When finished, he gave a nod of satisfaction.

'I can't believe it,' he said in amazement. 'A Mountie?

He come all this way . . . after us?'

'He still wore the bottom portion of his uniform, and there's no mistakin' them boots they wear.'

'A man like that – he makes our own US marshals look like amateurs.'

'Probably be a few days afore anyone finds the body,' Seevy said. 'But we might ought tuh find a cattle ranch nearby. We can split up and mix in our tracks with a few head of beeves – just in case anyone should try and track us from the dead Mountie.'

'There are several ranches between here and Rimrock. We'll continue due south for the time being. Once we enter a herd of range cattle, we'll turn to the west and ride single file. That should make it doubly hard for anyone to find or follow our tracks.'

'Noonan tried tuh paw the woman yesterday,' Seevy changed the subject. 'I dressed him down fer it, but he likes tuh manhandle women. You 'member the squaw we took in trade a coupla years back.'

'Yeah,' Stewart growled. 'When she fought back, the idiot broke her neck!'

'He's an animal when it comes tuh women – 'specially Indian women.'

'I keep telling you – Washta ain't no Indian! I took a peek at her washing at the stream a couple days back. Her legs are as white as yours or mine. She maybe forgot how to speak English, or she might even be a foreigner – French, Swede, German – who knows? The thing is, the woman ain't no regular squaw. If Noonan gets out of line with her again, I'll take a horse whip to him. You tell him that!'

'I'll tell him,' Seevy vowed. 'But when he gets something in his head. . . .'

He didn't have to finish. Stewart grunted. 'Yeah, the man's a hog-wild beast when it comes to females.'

'You want I should hang back tuh watch the rear?'

Stewart shook his head. 'No. Once we find enough cattle to erase our tracks, there won't be anyone who can figure out we went to Rimrock.'

'Good enough. Come sundown, I'll ride ahead fer enough to find us a place tuh camp tonight.'

'Glad to have you along, Seevy,' Stewart told him. 'You're the best man I ever worked with – and that includes my brothers.'

Seevy grinned. 'If you only had Eddie, I'd say that was no real compliment.' He laughed. 'But Quinn is a solid hand.'

Stewart laughed too. 'Little brothers – what can you do?'

'If they're like Eddie, you pick up after them fer the rest of your life.'

Jared and Cliff had joined with Shane to help him sort some horses. A couple of stallions had been running with this herd for a few weeks, so they needed to cull the young mares who might be carrying foal. They drove the herd into a box canyon, then took time to remove the stallions. After that, it was a rather tedious job of sorting the horses into the two groups.

Cliff, as usual, kept the conversation going with his tales of female conquest. Some of the stories were too wild to be believed, but Cliff had been on the disorderly side before he ended up living on the ranch. Now, saddled with an adopted child, he should have grown up, but he was fighting off maturity as if it was the plague.

'Gotta say, Jer,' Cliff spoke to Jared. 'You and Reese have become the old bachelors on the Valeron ranch. First Brett gets hitched, and now Nash has tied the knot . . . and both of them are your younger brothers!'

'You're the one with a child to raise, Cuz,' Jared retorted. 'If anyone needs a wife, it's you.'

'I've got plenty of time.'

'Nessy is quite fond of Veta,' Shane put in, having been silent during Cliff's ragging on Jared. 'A little girl needs a mother.'

'There's four Valeron girls already handling that job,' Cliff dismissed the notion. 'Nessy has a choice of older women to be close to.'

'Isn't the same as a real mother,' Jared spoke up. 'You're not even home to tuck her into bed some nights.'

'Tish takes care of that.'

Shane laughed and spoke to Jared. 'Yeah, but Sis charges him four bits every time she does. You remember how he whined and complained about how it cost him six dollars last month? And that's not counting the times he's had to pay to have her tended some days.'

'Didn't you say Tish was charging him a dollar a day for that?' Jared remarked to Shane. 'That means Cliff is working for about ten to fifteen dollars a month.'

'Yes, sir. My sister is putting together a right nice nest egg – and all at his expense!'

Cliff shrugged off the laughter of his two cousins. 'I'm still the youngest male relative on the ranch. I've got plenty of time . . . and plenty of gals just waiting for me to give them a whirl.'

'I'm glad of one thing,' Jared said. 'At least our sisters are safe from Cliff's womanizing ways. He ever tries to cuddle up to one of his cousins and Pa, Temple and Udal will kick his bucket right off of the ranch!'

'And where would that leave poor little Nessy?' Shane taunted Cliff. 'A man with fatherly responsibilities ought to be making a decent home for his child, not gallivanting all over the country, wooing one girl and then the next. Even your brother has settled down with one woman, and Rod didn't have an amorous bone in his whole body!'

'All right, all right!' Cliff lamented. 'Let's get down to the job at hand. I'm tired of you both ganging up on me all of the time.'

'Who started this by calling me and Reese old bachelors?' Jared fired back.

Shane held up a hand to stop any further exchange. 'Rider coming,' he said, pointing back down the valley. 'It looks like Wendy.'

'She rides like a man,' Jared bragged. 'Her and Scarlet are both good riders.'

'Coming fast,' Shane said. 'Must be trouble.'

As one, the three of them turned their horses away from the herd and rode to meet Jared's sister.

Wendy pulled her horse to a stop, breathing hard, winded from the ride. She waited until the three men had stopped before she gave them the news about Reese and the others finding a dying Mountie.

'Reese asks that you come at once, Jerry,' she said. 'He

and Landau will meet you – it's on the shortcut you told him about.'

'I remember.'

'What about Scarlet?' Shane wanted to know.

'She is going to stay with Nash until Jerry and Reese get this sorted out.'

'I'll go with you,' Shane volunteered.

'Me too,' Cliff joined in.

'You've got a child to take care of,' Wendy reminded him. 'A family man doesn't run off to risk his life when he has parental responsibilities.'

'Ah, for the love of. . . .'

'You're staying!' Jared informed him curtly.

'I'll send the Indian wranglers up to help get the mares separated. You keep the herd in the box canyon until they get here.'

'Takoda and Chayton don't even talk English around me.'

'If I was them,' Shane joked, 'I'd pretend I didn't understand English around you too. That way, they don't have to listen to you brag about all of the women you've known.'

'This really stinks,' Cliff whined. 'I never asked to become a father!'

'As I recall, you did just that,' Shane reminded him. 'You told Nessy you would look after her.'

'Yeah, but as her big brother, not a father!'

'I didn't hear you complaining when she started calling you daddy,' Jared countered.

Wendy displayed an impish simper. 'If you ever want to lessen the burden of fatherhood, you can always marry

Veta . . . or one of the other girls you claim are standing in line waiting their turn for your affection. If you remember, Martin went on the last undertaking with Jared – but he has a wife to watch over his two kids.'

Cliff raised his hands in a sign of surrender. 'OK, so I'm staying with the blasted horses! You Valerons go have a wild time, and I'll stay here and do this boring chore. But,' he added quickly, 'don't forget to send the Indians up to help me finish with these horses. I want to get home in time to put Nessy to bed. Tish is gonna break me!'

Nash contacted the carpenter who made the coffins, plus the local undertaker, and had them take charge of Brock Gordon's body. They laid the Mountie to rest a couple hours later and then Nash and Trina joined Reese, Landau and Scarlet for a meal at Castle Point's only restaurant.

'The last time I saw you, Reese,' Nash turned to normal conversation, 'was when you came to Denver to pick up my Gatling gun.'

Trina stared at him. 'You had a Gatling gun?'

Nash grinned. 'It was some months before I met you. I thought I'd told you about it. Some guy couldn't pay for my services and he gave me the gun for collateral. He never returned to pick it up. Reese needed an equalizer to take on the gunmen at Brimstone.'

'That was a bad time for us all,' Landau said tightly. 'I was busy guarding Scarlet.'

'This was supposed to be a fun trip,' Scarlet complained. 'Now, look at the chore we've got ahead of us.'

'Did you send a wire to Canada?' Nash asked Reese.

'I wired Brett with the pertinent information. He has the connections to get the telegraph message to the right people. I imagine it will take some time to reach their headquarters. I told him about the ambush and that we were looking into it. I promised to keep him informed of our progress.'

'Not much else the Mounties can do, but let us handle it,' Landau said. 'They don't cross our border and our troops don't cross theirs.'

'So sad,' Scarlet murmured. 'Brock lost his brother, and now he is dead too. And all because of the greed of a handful of ruthless whiskey dealers.'

'It's why Pa is so dead-set against drinking hard liquor,' Nash proclaimed. 'It does a lot more harm than good.'

'Sometimes,' Landau contended, 'life is more than a man can bear. I admit, I used the bottle to dull the pain of living for a time.'

'Yeah, but you got past it,' Reese defended him. 'Had you been part of a family – had someone else to turn to for counsel – you might not have needed to numb your brain.'

'And even when you were drinking, I'll bet you never reached a point where you would trade your wife or children for a jug of rotgut,' Nash added. 'Scarlet told us the Mountie claimed the Indians had done that on this very trip.'

'He did,' Reese confirmed. 'Two Indian children had been sold into slavery, but there was still a squaw with them, the wife of an Indian called Big Nose.'

'If they still have her with them, it should make them easier to follow,' Landau pointed out.

'If Jared got the wire, he should be headed this way,'

Nash changed the direction of their conversation. 'I imagine he'll bring one or two of the others along.'

'Landau and I will meet him at the ambush site,' Reese stated.

'There might only be the three of you,' Trina spoke up. 'You said there were at least six whiskey-traders!'

'These aren't gunmen,' Landau was the one to answer. 'They are lowlife, greedy skunks, who sell and trade their snake venom to the Indians. I've never heard of any whiskey dealers killing a Mountie before. It's bad for their trade.'

'Even so,' Scarlet sounded off her own concern, 'these men not only killed the two Mounties in Canada, they ambushed and killed Brock as well.'

Landau added, 'The killer left him to die on a remote strip of land. No way he could have known there would be anyone close enough to hear the gunshot. If we hadn't been taking that shortcut, we'd never have come across his body.'

'Meaning those fellows think they got away clean,' Reese reasoned. 'They won't be expecting anyone to know their names or be following.'

'They will still try and hide their trail,' Landau said. 'I speak from experience – never assume the law isn't on your back-trail.'

'It's why we sent for Jared,' Reese said. 'He's the best tracker in the family. Plus, we couldn't take after them with Scarlet – Pa would have strung both of us up by our heels.'

Landau put in, 'We also only had one day's provisions. Wyoming has a whole lot of open country. If them boys kept shy of any trading posts or towns, it might be several days before they passed by any place to get more supplies. We simply didn't have the means to start after them.'

'So how is your medical profession going, Doctor Valeron?' Scarlet changed the subject. 'And do you have an extra bed for your favorite sister, or should I get a room at the boarding house?'

'The addition to the house is complete,' Nash told her. 'We now have three patient rooms and a full-size bedroom for us. We also added an indoor pump to serve the kitchen and examination room, and installed a bathtub. We can heat the water in a small reservoir tank and have hot water available at any time.'

'Durned if you aren't getting spoiled,' Reese said. 'You get too many comforts, Ma and Pa will be coming for an extended visit.'

'It made all the difference, getting the extra money from the reward on those outlaws Jared and Wyatt turned over to the Denver police last year.'

'Well, if you've got room for Miss Scarlet,' Landau got back to their situation, 'it will make leaving her here much easier. Me and Reese hate to desert her in the middle of our trip.'

'I don't intend to stay here for who knows how long,' Scarlet responded with some vigour. 'If you're not back within a week, Landy, I'll go to Denver by myself.'

Landau could not prevent a sheepish expression at Scarlet using her pet name for him. She didn't care for the handle Landau, and had taken to using the nickname Landy. It was the first time she had used it except for when the two of them were alone.

Reese kept a straight face. 'Trust me, sis, you wouldn't have as much fun in Denver without *Landy*.'

'Trina could make the trip with her,' Nash volunteered, ignorant of Landau's plan to propose marriage. 'She could stand to do a little shopping.'

Reese scowled at his younger brother. 'Let's just see if we can't get this sorted out as quickly as possible.'

'One week, Landy,' Scarlet repeated. 'That's as long as I'll wait.'

CHAPTER THREE

Washta kept her eyes fixed on either her work or her feet, obeying every order given without complaint or even a nod of understanding. She knew Stewart had guessed she was not Indian, but she avoided saying a single word. Big Nose had cured her of ever questioning an order. After months of his physical abuse, Washta had learned to complete every project as quickly and silently as possible. Considering her captors, Washta evaluated them in her mind.

Stewart had a pompous air about him, slightly larger in build than Quinn. The two of them looked quite a bit alike, while Eddie was slight of build and had a weakness about his character. He dutifully accepted whatever his older brothers said. None of the three were anything to brag about – Quinn and Steward were rather heavy-set, with thick lips, wide noses and tawny-brown-colored hair. They didn't bathe often and all three wore handle-bar moustaches as if they were in competition with one another. Porky was pretty much harmless, while Seevy was a bewhiskered jackal, able to move without being seen, and seemed a man without a soul. Killing came as naturally to him as swatting a fly. Korkle was the least offensive, while Noonan embodied every decent woman's nightmare. A man obsessed with his black, wavy hair, he could molest her with a single glance, and the voracious hunger in his eyes warned how much he would take from a woman to slake his appetite.

Overall, her situation was not intolerable. The house had a closed-in back porch, and she had been provided with an old buffalo robe to place on the floor for a bed and a couple blankets for warmth. Stewart allowed her to eat in private, but sometimes stood or sat around and watched her working. The plus side, he had never struck her. Raising his voice was all it took if she lagged at a chore – and there were plenty of those. Cooking, cleaning, doing laundry and waiting on six or seven men continually – it was a daunting task. On this rare occasion, she was temporarily left without a mountain of work. She took a moment to sit in a chair on the porch. She gazed at the sparse clouds overhead, watched the occasional flutter of a bird, and enjoyed the feel of heat from the sun. Wyoming could get much hotter in summer than Canada, and the wind seemed to blow all the time. She had heard the men talk about how the winters could be very harsh, but it was a pleasant morning this day.

Considering her situation, it was preferable to the life she'd had with Big Noose and living in the Indian encampment. She didn't have to gather firewood and Stewart didn't expect her to chew the fat from animal skins to make the hides softer and more malleable for moccasins or clothing. There was a roof over her head, though there were numerous drafts from the cracks in the walls of her tiny room, but it was private. If the men continued to let her alone, it would be a vast improvement over serving Big Nose.

Even as she sagged back in the chair to relax, Korkle and Noonan rode up to the front of the house. They had spent the night in town gambling and drinking. Korkle had grey in his seldom-groomed hair and was the oldest member of the gang, while Noonan appeared to be in his mid-twenties. At present, both men bore the red eyes caused from lack of sleep and too much drink.

'Hey, sweet-cake!' Noonan chirped a greeting. 'You look to have settled in real good.'

Korkle added a rare remark, 'Bet that's the first time she's sat in a proper chair since she can remember.'

'We ought to keep a blanket on the porch!' Noonan chortled inanely. 'She could sit cross-legged like a normal squaw.'

Their arrival ended Washta's short respite. She rose to return to the kitchen.

'Don't go running off!' Noonan said quickly. 'How about you and me take a walk together? There ain't no woods closer than where we put in the still, but we could sure enough inspect a couple pinyon trees or flowering cactus.'

Washta ignored the offer and hurried her step, entering the modest house and leaving the two men chuckling about her quick exit.

'You got no more chance with that gal than a hayseed in a tornado, Noonan,' she heard Korkle razz the younger man.

'She'll come around,' was Noonan's confident reply. 'Them Injun gals like to play it coy, but they are the same as any other woman. I'll bet I could have Washta panting for me in about five minutes flat.'

Korkle uttered a cynical laugh. 'Yeah, she'd be panting – 'cause you had to run her down like a spooked fawn!'

A cloud of dread settled like a heavy shroud upon Washta's shoulders as she entered the kitchen. She seldom washed her hair or face. Her clothes were a buckskin skirt that reached her ankles and a heavy woolen blouse that hid her feminine form. She washed carefully when completely alone, but had not laundered her outfit – it was gamy and wholly uninviting. Yet, nothing deterred Noonan's interest. Stewart had promised that, if she was good and did her chores, no one would bother her. However, she was terrified of Noonan. Washta presented a challenge to him. To possess her would be a measure of triumph for his insatiable appetite. One day soon, he would catch her by herself and then. . . .

Washta began to peel potatoes for the stew she would serve the men for their next meal. Her hands did the work automatically, while her mind turned over ideas and options. She knew there was a town nearby, a place called Rimrock, but she had no allies there. In fact, she had heard the men laughing about the friendship and protection they had cultivated with the local law and the all-important people in town. She would find no help there. The next closest town was Broken Spoke, but it was a full day's ride – two or more days if on foot. She couldn't hope to make such a journey without getting caught.

With no alternatives, she decided she would bide her

time. If Stewart and the others grew comfortable enough around her – believing she had accepted her situation – they might grow careless. If she somehow ended up alone for a day or even a few hours, she might be able to acquire a horse. A little food and water, plus a good horse, and she would strike out for Cheyenne. They had soldiers and lawmen there. She could report the deaths of the three Mounties and perhaps get some help. It was a near hopeless plan, but what else could she do?

It took a half-day for Jared to scout around and locate the tracks of the whiskey dealers. Once away from the grazing herd of cattle, the tracks were clear.

'They are confident no one would find their trail,' Jared spoke to Reese. 'Looks like a half-dozen or more horses – including some bigger, draft animals. It appears as if the riders are headed towards Rimrock.'

'Fair-sized town,' Landau spoke up. 'I worked with a man who once spent a few months working in a coal mine over that way. He said they shipped quite a bit of coal from Rimrock.'

'I was there a time or two, trading horses,' Shane joined in. 'I remember they had a town sheriff and jail. It's a busy place.'

'That could make this easy,' Reese said hopefully. 'We get the law to arrest these men and we will have done our duty.'

Jared snorted his cynicism. 'We have nothing but the word of a dying man, big brother. Other than a couple of his possessions and his horse, we can't prove a thing.'

'We find the Indian squaw and that will prove they are

dealing whiskey to the Indians,' Landau chipped in. 'That's against the law.'

'Except the Indians aren't in this country,' Jared continued his pessimism. 'Our only shot will be claiming the guy told us who ambushed him. However, Brock only said it was one of the men who worked with the whiskey dealers. Far as a judge and jury goes, it could have been any outlaw or renegade who wanted to rob him, or maybe thought he was after them.'

Reese said, 'OK, Jared. I can see this is going to be a tough sell. Do you have a better idea?'

'When the law can't or won't act, it's up to the people themselves to deal out justice. That's all I'm saying. If you and Landau are sincere about this, we might end up doing it outside the local law.'

'Only as a last resort,' Reese rebuked his statement. 'Those men still have a hostage. Brock said it was the wife of Big Nose. If she isn't happy with her situation, she might be of some help.'

'Who'd take the word of a squaw?' Shane asked. 'I mean, if she is unhappy about being traded for a jug of firewater, she might say anything to be rid of these guys.' He harrumphed. 'I'm not saying I wouldn't believe her – just pointing out what a judge and jury might think.'

Reese posited, 'We'll talk to the law first off. If we get no help from them, then we can try talking to the Indian woman.'

'And if we get nothing?' Jared asked, eyeing his brother with an expectant look.

'Miss Scarlet made that Mountie a promise,' Landau answered for Reese. 'I reckon we will do whatever is necessary to see her promise is kept.'

'Hear, hear,' Shane went along with him. 'If Cousin Scarlet believed the dying man and gave her word, that's good enough for me.'

'We need to spend a couple days gathering more wood,' Quinn told Stewart. 'Porky stuck by the ranch and tended the horse herd while we were gone, same as usual. Even so, the work around here and up at the still is way behind. Without adequate firewood, it'll delay starting up the still. We need to get things going. We've got the mash, and the water is running good in the stream, yet we know the creek sometimes goes dry in late summer. If we want to get six barrels of whiskey ready for our next trip, we need to step things up.'

Stewart nodded. Porky was mentally a little slow on the draw, but he minded as well as a trained dog. 'You fixed the condenser and cleaned out the deposits from the copper vat and doubler?'

'Everything is ready. I even cleaned the burner to make sure we can maintain an even heat.'

'Something sure went wrong with that one batch. We can't be killing or blinding our customers – it's bad for business.'

'Not to mention our own health,' Quinn cautioned. 'Big Nose was on his way to kill us. If those two Mounties hadn't shown up first. . . .' He didn't have to finish.

'We'll cut the chief a special price if he's still around,' Stewart dismissed the last misunderstanding. 'Who knows? Big Nose might have been run out of the country by the Mounties. There's a good chance they blamed him and his people for the deaths of those two mounted police.'

'Except for Frost and our wagons being there.'

'Far as anyone knows, the Mounties might have tried to stop the Indians,' Stewart explained a logical scenario.

Quinn grunted and returned to business. 'The rest of the stuff we ordered should be in town by now. I thought you and Seevy could pick up the order, while I take Eddie and Korkle out to the still. It will take at least three of us to get things in operation.' He grunted a second time. 'And Porky ain't much help on that end of things.'

'What's Noonan doing?'

'He has to rebuild the wagon we bought so it will hold the weight.'

'Maybe we should have picked out a bigger rig, one more heavy-duty to start with?'

'You know what that would mean, Stu – a team of at least eight horses, instead of four. Plus, it would look suspicious as hell, driving around a covered freight wagon that size.' He shrugged. 'Not to mention it would slow us down to a crawl. Tough enough to feed and care for four draft animals on these trips.'

'All right, I guess it makes more sense to add those heavy support braces and carry two extra wheels for breakdowns.'

'Noonan is the only one with blacksmith experience. If not for him, I'd have never managed to build the still by myself.'

'I just hate leaving him here alone.' He lowered his voice, 'you know, with Washta.'

Quinn understood. 'I could take her with me? She could help round up firewood.'

'Porky is handling that, and she might decide to disappear in those woods. Wouldn't do to have her run off.'

'Well, you're going to have to make it clear to Noonan that he is to keep his hands off of her,' Quinn said firmly. 'We need to make a lot of money on this next trip. Tell him, if he messes with the squaw, we will boot him off of the crew. That ought to keep him in line.'

'We could put off the fixing of the wagon.'

'Not if we want to get the load of coal up here. It's getting impossible to find enough fuel for our stove here at the house. And I hate to use any of the firewood we gather for the still. We have to keep that mash at 175 degrees twenty-four hours a day. It's bad enough someone has to sit and watch the still day and night, but there's no time for gathering extra wood. A man leaves for a few minutes and the fire might die down or the catching bucket might overflow – even the water level might drop and we lose the condenser.' Quinn shook his head. 'No, we've got to buy fuel for this place and the guy at the coal yard said they were running low. Seems there was a cave-in or something that is slowing the mining operation. He expects they are going to run out of product before the mining gets going good again.'

'You're the brains for the still, Quinn,' Stewart admitted. 'You call the shots when it comes to brewing the liquor we need. Soon as the wagon is ready, we'll pick up the coal. Then we can park it out at the still so we can fill the barrels and not have to load them into the bed by hand.'

'That's a good idea,' his brother agreed.

'And don't worry, I'll speak to Noonan . . . and also tell

Washta to keep her distance while we're gone.'

'You've got your trails mixed up,' Sheriff Donovan declared firmly. 'Porky has been coming in every week for supplies, same as always. Ain't no way the Macreedys could have spent several weeks up in Canada. Shucks, that's a two-week ride! Besides, they sell a herd of horses at the Denver auction every fall. Them boys have been busy gathering and breaking wild mustangs since the first green of spring.'

'They go all the way to Denver to sell their horses?' Jared queried. 'I'd think Cheyenne would be a whole lot closer.'

Donovan shrugged. 'Guess they get a better price in Denver than from the military in Cheyenne.'

'We tracked them from the site of the ambush all the way to their ranch,' Reese insisted. 'The dying Mountie said they were selling liquor to the Indians, and also sold a couple of Indian girls.'

Donovan was past his prime, portly built, with trimmed white hair, and a thick mustache. He used a deputy on weekends, or when he had a prisoner, but otherwise did his job alone. He seemed a man who didn't like to stir the pot when things were simmering nicely on their own.

'I'm a town sheriff, boys,' he said, wanting to end the conversation. 'And, even if – and I ain't taking a position on this – if the Macreedys were guilty of these things, there ain't no law in Wyoming against selling whiskey to Indians in a foreign country.'

'What about Brock Gordon?' Jared wanted to know. 'He was killed not fifty miles from here.'

'*Town sheriff!*' Donovan repeated emphatically. 'You got no witnesses and it ain't in my jurisdiction.'

'How about informing the US Marshal's office?' Landau wanted to know.

'Feel free if you've a mind,' he said. 'But – and you can trust me on this – I don't see that anyone is gonna arrest the Macreedys for murder. Them fellers never cause an ounce of trouble . . . and they usually pay their bills and taxes on time. Can't say that for a good many of the small ranches or farmers in this neck of the woods.'

'And this guy, Porky?' Reese queried. 'He claims those men have been here for the past two or three months?'

'I asked him how things were going just last week,' Donovan answered. 'He said a couple of the boys were down with a nasty cold, but they were on the mend.'

'These guys don't happen to have an Indian woman working for them?'

Donovan frowned. 'I couldn't say. I ain't been out to their ranch since they bought it from the bank. I do know they had a Mexican gal working for them for a few months last winter, but she left to be with some of her family a while back.'

Jared and Reese exchanged looks, both reaching the same conclusion – there would be no help from the local law. This investigation was up to them.

'We need to rest our horses,' Reese spoke to the sheriff. 'Reckon we will stick around a day or two. That all right with you?'

'Shore 'nuff,' Donovan said, glad the interrogation was behind him. 'The hotel is first class, and we've got a couple good eating places too.'

The three of them left the office and joined up with Shane, who had remained with the horses.

'No help, huh?' Shane said, seeing their long faces.

'We'll have to do this on our own,' Jared told him.

'If we do any riding, we'll have to rent horses,' Shane told him. 'Our animals need a couple day's rest and some decent feed.'

'Let's visit the livery,' Reese said. 'We'll take care of the horses and pick out a couple rentals. Then, we will get ourselves a couple rooms and discuss our next move over a meal.'

Washta suffered a sense of dreaded anticipation. The workload was difficult and she barely managed six or seven hours sleep nightly. With men going and coming, she seldom had a moment's peace. But now, everyone was gone from the house except for Noonan – sometimes called 'Slick', because he used something called Macassar oil to keep his hair in place. Washta had seen the packaging. It consisted of coconut oil, palm oil and oil from flowers called 'ylang-ylang'. She had never heard of such a flower, but the advertisement on the container promised to strengthen and stimulate hair growth while keeping shaggy hair in place.

She had overheard Noonan bragging to the others about his manly prowess with the ladies. Washta figured the term '*ladies*' was distinctly incorrect. Soiled doves, dance-hall girls or paid companions without morals, would have been more accurate. Nothing about the man's overbearing and lecherous personality would have attracted a proper woman. Trapped with such a man, alone, vulnerable . . . it had her stomach tied in knots.

As it was a laundry day, Washta was busy with a washtub and scrub-board. Once the clothing was wrung out as much as possible, she would take the laundry basket out back and hang the clothes over the duel clothesline. It was a makeshift cord, which ran between the house and the shed, as there were no trees nearby, and no one had put in the time or effort to plant posts for something so seldom used – previous to her arrival, at least.

She was on the last batch of clothes when Noonan took a break from his work on the freight wagon. Washta had felt his eyes on her many times, but he had only gotten frisky once during their travels. Stewart had warned him off after that. Today, however, the man was emboldened by no one else being on the place. As she carried the basket out to the clothesline, he sauntered over and blocked her path.

'You know,' the sleazy womanizer drawled, 'you wouldn't be half-bad to look at, if you didn't hide your face under that stringy hair, and kept up the appearance of a street beggar.'

Washta did not look him in the face. She attempted a side-step to go around him, but the man moved again to obstruct her way.

'I know some Indian girls do that,' he continued to taunt her. 'They smear paint on their faces and try to hide their wares with loose clothing – hoping to keep young, amorous bucks at a distance.' He snorted sarcastically. 'But they are girls in their teens, who don't wish to be married yet, or given to one of the dirty old men in the tribe. You sure ain't no spring chicken.'

Washta's heart began to pound with apprehension and she backed up a step. Noonan had a sneer on his lips and lust glowed brightly within his eyes. This time there would be no one to stop him from doing as he pleased. She looked around quickly, hoping to spot a weapon of some kind. Life had not been kind to her, so she had no fear of death. The only thing she could cling to was being left alone. If she couldn't have that much satisfaction out of living, she would die protecting her modesty.

Washta had not made a sound since being taken – she did not cry out now. Noonan knocked the basket out of her hands and caught hold of her arms. Before he could pull her to him, she began to fight against the far-bigger man with all of her might.

Noonan was strong and he batted away her flying fists. He leapt forward and encircled her in his arms, hugging her tight against his chest.

'Go ahead and fight,' he panted, struggling mightily to control her. 'You're not going to deny me what I want!'

Washta tried to kick, but the brute held her so close she couldn't get any leverage. He pushed her backwards until she banged against the wall of the house. With her pinned and helpless, he tried to force a kiss from her. When she denied his attempt by turning her head away, he drove a fist into her stomach, knocking both the fight and the wind out of her.

'You've got no virtue to protect!' he snarled. 'Relax, sweet-cake! Relax and enjoy it!'

CHAPTER FOUR

Washta struggled uselessly, pinned snugly against the side of the building, trying to suck air into her lungs, and completely powerless to stop Noonan from having his way with her. Then, abruptly, the sleazy, would-be rapist ceased his attack. Washta risked a glance at his face and saw his mouth was open and his eyes were glazed. Without uttering a word, his knees buckled and he dropped straight to the ground. Standing behind Noonan was a stranger, holding a gun in his hand. He had evidently struck her assailant on the back of the head with it.

'How about *you* relax, Mr Wannabe Romeo,' the man muttered to the unconscious heap at her feet. When he lifted his gaze, a smile spread across his face. As calm as you please, he asked, 'Would you be the lady of this here house?'

Before she could answer, a second man appeared, having come around from the front of the house. The similarity between the two was quite striking, although this second man looked a little older than the one who had clouted Noonan.

'What are you doing, Jer?' the new arrival asked in an exasperated tone of voice. 'Did you cold-cock that fellow?'

'This lowlife coyote punched the lady here, Reese,' her rescuer replied, holstering his weapon. 'A man starts mistreating a woman or child. . . .' He shrugged his shoulders. 'You know how I feel about that sort of thing.'

'Ma'am?' Reese asked, his face showing an immediate concern. 'Are you injured?'

She placed a hand over her tender stomach, but managed to turn her head slightly from side to side. It was only then she noticed that Noonan had torn her dress enough that one shoulder was partially exposed. She hurriedly pulled the material up into place.

'Are you the only two people on the place?' Reese asked her.

Another simple nod.

'What do you think?' the one called Jer said. 'She's tan, dark hair and dressed like an Indian. She has to be the one Brock told us about.'

Reese showed an instant compassion, moving over to take her by the arm. 'Come inside, ma'am,' he coaxed. 'We can sit down so you can collect your senses. Something to drink will help you get settled.'

Washta allowed him to lead her back through the rear door, while Jer removed Noonan's gun and began to drag the swine toward the tool shed.

Reese sat Washta down at the table and poured her some water from a nearby pitcher. Then he handed her the cup and took the chair across from her. She took a sip or two, curious about why the two men had come.

'Seems to me that you could use some new clothes,'

Reese commented, appraising her ragged outfit. 'Looks like you've been living and sleeping in that outfit so long it's nearly threadbare in a good many places.'

She took a moment to examine her attire, oddly concerned for the first time in ages as to her appearance. Moving a hand up to brush a strand of hair from her face, she was painfully aware of how dirty she was – clothing, body and hair.

'My name is Reese Valeron,' the man introduced himself. 'Me and my brother, Jared, have been tracking the Macreedy boys. We believe they killed a Mountie a few days back, and are responsible for the death of two more Mounties and several Indians up in Canada.'

Washta moistened her lips, wondering what these two brothers could do against seven men.

'Now,' Reese continued, 'the last Mountie they shot – he was barely alive when we found him. He said there was an Indian woman with the band of killers. Would you be that woman?'

Washta lowered her head, suffering a renewed shame. Before she had been taken, she had heard stories about other captive women and girls. They were never returned in chaste condition and few ever escaped their disgrace. Many took their own lives – either during captivity or shortly afterwards.

'Are you the one?' he asked again, when she delayed answering. 'Would you be. . . .' he corrected the question and asked: '*Were you* Big Nose's woman?'

She resigned herself to cooperate and gave a slight nod of her head.

Reese eyed her critically. 'Forgive me for being blunt,

but, from the light-colored skin I noticed on your bare shoulder, I don't believe you are an Indian.'

She said nothing.

'We Valerons are a law-abiding, God-loving family,' he informed her. 'When necessary, we have sought out justness for serious crimes. Me and Jared have two other brothers, one of which is a town sheriff. He used to be a US Marshal, so we have some allies in the judicial system. We don't aim to allow these men to get away with murder and the selling or enslaving of Indian girls.'

Still nothing.

He was persistent. 'Washta – means pretty or something like that, don't it?'

She avoided eye contact, staring at the cup of water.

'Listen, lady,' Reese's voice remained gentle, but his tone was firm. 'It's plain to see that you've had a bad time of it. But me and my brother are here to help. We can get you back to your family, or help you start your life anew in any town or city you choose. But we are going to need your help to put these men behind bars.'

Washta continued her silence, but drew her brows slightly together in deep thought. Here was her chance to get away from the Macreedys. These men seemed decent and caring. All she had to do was speak up.

'One thing more,' Reese added earnestly. 'No one in our family ever assigns blame to an innocent victim. We followed these men to Rimrock to see justice is done for the murder of three good men, and for the other atrocities they have committed. I believe you are a victim, not in any way responsible for your current predicament.'

Her lips parted, but she had been mute for so long. She

wondered if her voice still worked.

'I admit that trusting a stranger – after what you've been through – is not easy,' Reese went on with his entreaty. 'But I assure you, the word of a Valeron is as sacred as the words in the Holy Bible.'

Washta gave a slight 'ahem' to signal her surrender. It also reminded her vocal cords how to function.

'I believe you,' she said hoarsely, the sound of her words oddly foreign to her own ears. Taking another sip of water to slake the dryness of her unused throat, she began to confide her story to Reese.

'About two years ago, I lost my entire family in an Indian raid. I was taken captive, and after a time, ended up as Big Nose's woman.'

'I'm right sorry,' Reese said gently.

She went on, suddenly eager to have her history in the open. 'Big Nose was a brutal taskmaster and I learned to obey him without question. When he drank, he was worse.'

'How did you end up with the Macreedys?'

'Big Nose traded me for a jug of liquor.'

'Brock – the Mountie we found – said there were a couple children too.'

'Yes,' she swallowed back a sob at the memory, 'but the poor little girls were sold to a man while we were still in Montana. I wish. . . .' She paused, unable to speak for a moment. Remembering their imploring faces, the tears, the way they clung to her – it was too much to bear.

'Take your time,' Reese coaxed.

Washta sniffed to prevent tears and bolstered up the courage to finish. 'The Macreedys kept me to do their cooking, cleaning and housekeeping. They promised I would not be... taken advantage of.'

'Then the guy Jared clubbed – he acted on his own, against orders.'

She nodded.

'How about the Mounties? Did you witness any of the murders?'

'I was at the campsite when the two MPs showed up. Eddie Macreedy – he's the youngest of the three brothers – he started shooting and a couple of the hired men joined in. One of those men was wounded severely during the shootout and the Mounted Police were both killed. Big Nose and some braves were supposedly on their way to attack the camp – something about some bad liquor that caused the death of a couple of his people. The Macreedys left their wounded man to die and made a run for the border. They also left a wagon and a lot of supplies and such behind.'

'How about this other Mountie, the one who followed you? Do you know who killed him?'

'It was Seevy; he acts as a scout. I overheard him telling Stewart about shooting a man who had been on our trail, but I didn't see it.'

'Darn!' Reese did not hide his dejection. 'We could have used a first-hand account. The local sheriff is not inclined to do anything about what happened in Canada. It would seem the Macreedys have garnered some support around town, so he prefers to remain ignorant of their crimes.'

'What does that mean . . . for me?' she asked hesitantly. 'I can only testify to what I heard Seevy say. That won't do much to convince a judge as to the guilt of these men.'

'First thing, we're taking you to town with us. We'll keep you safe until we figure a way to settle with the Macreedys.'

'There are six of them, besides the man who watches the house when they are gone. Two of you against seven men, plus the sheriff?'

Reese didn't have to answer as Jared entered the room in time to hear her statement. The younger-looking brother laughed. 'Missy, you don't know us Valerons. When one of us gets in a fix, we keep adding numbers or guns until we balance the scales.'

'It does sound like we are going to have trouble getting the law on our side,' Reese spoke to Jared. 'The lady here didn't see Brock Gordon at all. She only heard one of the men talking about the shooting.'

'You have the man's dying word – and Scarlet's promise,' Jared countered. 'That's enough for me.'

'If you recall, Jer, it's always been our custom to have the law on our side. We are going to need the US Marshal's office to back us up on any arrests.'

'Reese,' Jared said, his countenance grim, 'these men killed three Canadian Mounties. They've been selling whiskey to the Indians, and taking women and children in trade. Look at this unfortunate gal – they brought her here to be their personal slave. If we can't get a judge and jury to hang them for their crimes, I'm fine with us doing it ourselves.'

'First, we'll try it the legal route,' Reese replied. 'If all else fails. . . .' He sighed. 'Well, we've got some strings we can pull. Brett will know who to contact about . . . what's the term for sending someone back to another country to face their crimes? I believe Martin spoke of it one time.'

'*Extradition* is the word he used,' Jared told him. 'But them Mounties would be just as happy to get a letter saying justice was served right here.'

Reese laughed. 'Now I see why Brett has always claimed you would make a terrible deputy. You are too eager to be judge, jury and executioner.'

Jared grinned. 'Think of the time, energy and legal haggling saved by handling the process in one simple hanging. After all, if a man's guilty of murder and selling women and children, why spend months or even years getting him to the gallows?'

'What do you want me to do?' Washta asked quietly.

Reese showed a determined look. 'Big Nose made you his prisoner, and these men took you in trade for whiskey. To my way of thinking, you don't owe any of them anything but contempt. You aren't going to be anyone's slave. Like I said, we'll put you up at the hotel or a boarding house until this is settled.'

'But the Macreedys! They will come for me!'

'Lady,' Jared spoke to her, his voice laced with a dire assurance. 'As of here and now, you are under our protection. Anyone comes looking to take you against your will – it'll be the last mistake they ever make.'

Rather than take Washta to the hotel, Reese chose an establishment named Harmon House. It offered room and board, plus had heated baths or showers – conveniently afforded by a local hot springs. Reese expected there might be some discord about taking on a boarder who looked like an Indian squaw, so he entered ahead of the lady.

Ella Harmon ran the boarding house with her husband, Carl. He had been an engineer for twenty years and they built the place to provide for them a modest retirement. Ella was stoutly built, but had a warmth about her that put a person at ease. Quick to smile, Reese was reminded of his Aunt Faye, who was one of those people with a giving nature and made friends with everyone who met her.

Reese passed idle conversation to learn the background of the Harmons, then explained a little about Washta. Once finished, he introduced her to the landlady and asked about boarding and a bath.

'Girl,' Ella spoke to Washta, 'after one of our heated baths, you're going to look and feel ten years younger and a whole lot more like the white woman you are.' Then she gave her head a critical shake. 'If you don't mind, I'll toss those rags you're wearing in the trash.'

'That'll be fine,' Reese spoke up. 'While she is bathing, I'll go over to the general store and pick her up some clothes to replace that Indian garb.'

'Know a lot about buying for a lady, do you?' Ella pinned him down.

'Uh, well . . .'

She laughed. 'Soon as Carl has her bath ready, I'll go with you. There's a few things a lady needs that most unmarried men don't know nothing about.'

'I'll be in your debt, Mrs Harmon.'

'Toss in an extra two-bits for my help and we'll call it even.'

Reese stepped aside as Ella directed her attention to Washta. She opened a book that was sitting on a piece of furniture that looked like a church pulpit. Next to it on the wall was a row of keys with room numbers marked above each hook.

'And what's your proper name, hon?' she asked, picking up a pencil.

'It's Marie Singleton,' Washta surrendered her true title. 'I haven't used it for a long time.'

'Well, Marie,' Ella said. 'You best get used to being back in the civilized world. You're too young to be brooding or cursing the ill-fate you've suffered. Got to leave it all behind – like the dirt and grime you're going to wash off with our sweet-smelling soap. Once you're clean, with your hair fixed up, and wearing a new outfit, you'll feel like a proper lady again.'

'I don't know about that, but I do look forward to being clean once more.' She looked back at Reese and asked, somewhat timorously, 'You aren't leaving me?'

'No, miss,' he replied. 'I've a hankering to see what you look like underneath all the Indian garb. If you'd allow, I thought you might like to join my companions and me to discuss our overall situation during a meal at a nearby restaurant.'

Marie gave him a half-smile. 'I'd like that.'

'We provide two meals a day with the room,' Ella interjected. 'Breakfast is toast, eggs and ham – with mush on Sundays. We don't serve lunch, but supper is a full spread, served at six to six-thirty, seven nights a week. It's a bargain at a dollar-and-a-half daily. If you only want a room, that's a dollar a day.'

'She'll take room and board,' Reese advised Ella. 'And provide her a bath as often as she likes.' He took a double-eagle out of his pocket and set it next to the book Ella had used to register the new guest. 'This should cover things for a few days.'

'My kind of customer,' Ella laughed. 'I'll take the lady back to the dressing room and tell my husband to fill the tub. With the hot springs right under our back porch, we never have to heat water, and the whole place stays warm in the winter without needing fuel for anything but the cook stove.'

'Pays to marry an engineer,' Reese commented.

'Be back in a jiff, and you and I will go do some shopping. I'll get her foot size and measure her a bit, so don't get skittish and bolt for the hills.'

'I'll wait right here,' he promised.

Jared glared at the sheriff and hissed his anger through clenched teeth. 'She was there when they gunned down two North West Mounted Police! She also overheard the man called Seevy admit to the killing of Brock Gordon, the Mountie we buried on the trail. What more do you need?'

'I told you!' Donovan growled back. 'Nothing that happened in Canada means a thing here in Wyoming. And Porky can claim them boys never left the ranch. When faced with those facts, all you have is the word of an angry ex-squaw, who could be trying to get even with the men who traded whiskey for her. You go tell this to the judge and see what he says, but I can save you the trouble – you're wasting your time.'

'I see where your loyalty lies, Sheriff,' Jared said thickly. 'Money talks louder than victims!'

'You keep pushing me, young fella, and you're going to

see the inside of this here jail.'

Jared laughed at his threat. 'Trust me when I say, you don't want to do anything that foolish, Donovan. Wearing a local sheriff's badge don't mean a blessed thing when you're on the wrong side of the law. You can hide your head in a barrel over this, but don't threaten me. If we have to do your job for you, the safest thing for you is keep out of our way.'

The sheriff puffed up like a river frog, but he was wise enough to not push the issue. He knew the Valeron reputation and wasn't eager to test their convictions. With his jaw set and lips sealed tightly, he didn't say another word, as Jared left his office.

Once on the street, Jared located the telegraph office. He needed to let Nash know where they were at, so Scarlet wouldn't be worried. Then, he would send a wire to his father... and also Brett. As an ex-US Marshal, he could advise them on what steps they should take.

'Who were they?' Stewart roared. 'Who would dare come here and steal our housekeeper?'

'I never seen him before,' Noonan replied. 'Like I told you, the guy hit me from behind. By the time I come to, he was shutting the door on the shed. I only seen him through the cracks.'

'But there were two of them?'

'Yeah. They put Washta on a horse with one of them and left me locked up.'

'How come you didn't see them arrive?' Quinn wanted to know.

'I told you, I was busy working on the wagon and they

come up behind me.'

Seevy snorted at his lie. 'The tracks of them draggin' you is from back of the house, where Washta was hangin' out laundry. The laundry is still sittin' in the basket, instead of hangin' on the line.'

Noonan grimaced at Seevy's deduction. 'All right!' he snapped. 'I was having a little fun with the squaw.'

'Fun?' Stewart challenged.

'It was harmless enough,' Noonan maintained. 'I figured to coax a kiss out of her – all right? It was nothing!'

'You had a woman on your mind instead of keeping an eye on things,' Quinn accused. 'Now she's gone... and she knows we killed those Mounties!' He swore. 'You and your dog-in-heat impulses have put us in a real bind.'

Stewart held up a hand to stop any further bickering or blame. 'What we need to do now is figure out how to correct this problem before it comes back to bite us.'

'Want me tuh go into town and see what Washta is gonna do?' Seevy suggested.

'Yes, but don't try anything on your own. We'll leave Porky out at the still with Eddie. That will make five of us to handle the two kidnappers.'

'If the gal talks,' Quinn said, looking anxious, 'We might have to deal with Donovan.'

'The sheriff knows not to cross us. We pay taxes and add a lot of revenue to Rimrock. He won't take a squaw's word over ours.' Stewart bobbed his head with confidence. 'Besides, Porky has been buying supplies every week and telling the storekeeper about our progress with our new herd of horses. With the list of details I gave him to use, no one can prove we weren't on the ranch, catching and breaking mustangs the last couple months.'

'Got to admit, Stu, that was a great idea,' Quinn praised his planning. 'We stick to the roundup story and no one can say different.'

'We've still got the string of horses we grabbed in Colorado down in the lower pasture,' Seevy agreed. 'Only about twenty of them, but it's enough that we can pass for regular horse dealers.'

'This horse ranch has been a perfect cover,' Stewart declared. 'We can't risk anyone ruining our set-up.'

Quinn said, 'I'll ride out and get Korkle. I'll also let Eddie know what's going on.'

'It'll be dark by the time you get back,' Stewart surmised. 'Seevy, you go ahead and ride into town. See what you can find out – spend the night at the hotel if necessary. We'll all meet here for breakfast at sun-up and decide what needs to be done.'

CHAPTER FIVE

Marie stared at the image in the mirror with a fixed fascination. A vague memory of the oddly familiar reflection floated through the nether regions of her mind, like a long-forgotten memory that suddenly flashes through a person's head. Peering intently at the woman before her, she perceived the once youthful features that had made her slightly above average in looks. The eyes were more truthful – static, yet harboring the pain, indignation, and the ostensibly endless suffering of her captivity. Also, a perceivable uncertainty lingered just beneath the surface, evidence of her loss of freedom and independent actions or thoughts. The endless months of bondage, grief and toil without hope had left its mark.

'And now you have your life back,' she murmured to herself, as if saying the words aloud would help to remove the stigma and abasement of the past two years.

The door opened to her room and Ella fluttered in like a pet dove. She was a full-of-life person, more beautiful inside than out, with a natural mother-instinct that helped put Marie at ease.

'Why, the dress fits just fine!' Ella raved. 'My goodness! You look like a completely different person. I thought I must have entered the wrong room when I saw you standing before the mirror.'

'The person I see is something of a stranger to me too,' Marie replied. 'I don't know how I can ever thank you.'

'Tut, tut, hon,' Ella chirped in a sing-song voice. 'My dear, you have endured what no genteel woman should ever have to face. One time, a few years back, we had two female Indian hostages arrive in town with a contingent of soldiers. The one was missing most of her nose – you know that's a punishment or purposeful disfigurement to humiliate a woman – and the other had completely lost her mental faculties. I kept track of them for a bit. They both ended up in an asylum for those who had lost their way in the world. Neither of them were able to deal with the civilized world. You are so much more fortunate than they were . . . and I'd guess it's because you are much stronger.'

'I never felt very strong,' Marie admitted. 'More than once I searched for a way to end my life.'

Ella moved over and gave her a warm hug. When she stepped back she cooed, 'You're safe and sound now, hon. Carl and I know a little about the Valerons – they have a town named after them a day's ride from here.'

'I'm not real familiar with Wyoming. I was taken from our farm in Nebraska and passed along between several tribes until I ended up in Canada.'

'Can I help you with anything?' Ella wanted to know.

'No. Thank you so much for picking out the clothes – even the ribbon for my hair goes nicely with the outfit.'

'Well, Reese Valeron is waiting for you downstairs. I

must say, he seems a very gentlemanly sort. Dresses up right smartly too. Not the most handsome man around, but he has a very capable look about him.' She laughed. 'But, after having a look at Jared and Shane Valeron, I suspect everyone in that family is capable.'

Marie felt a renewed bout of nerves. She practically trembled at the thought of presenting herself as a lady. She had done everything she could to downplay her femininity and hide any attractive features for so long. . . .

'I guess I'm as ready as I'll ever be,' she said, biting her lip. 'I feel like a teenage girl being courted for the first time.'

'My advice,' Ella offered, 'just smile and let the men fawn over you.'

'Yeah . . . right,' Marie countered. She had been an Indian squaw and the bartered-for housekeeper to a bunch of whiskey-dealing slavers. How could a decent man ever get past that?

Dismissing the notion and attempting to quell her raging anxiety, Marie took a deep breath and exited her room.

Reese's face lit up when he saw her. He didn't do anything silly, like whistle or spew out words of flattery. Instead, he smiled and looked her over appreciatively. The action was far more ingratiatory than anything he could have said.

'Dressed up proper,' he said, shyly taking her hand, 'I doubt the Macreedys would even recognize you.'

'It has been a long time since I felt truly clean. I must have soaked for an hour or more.'

'Did you good,' he said. 'You look as fresh and alive as

a month-old colt.'

She smiled. 'Easy to see you come from a ranch. Even your flattery lends itself to your line of work.'

'Well, we do have a lot more than horses and cattle on the Valeron ranch, Miss Singleton. But comparing you to a sheep, goat, or some other animal didn't really seem fitting.'

She managed a slight smile for his effort to put her at ease. Then he led her out of the boarding house. The sun was down, but it wasn't yet dark. As they walked along the city street to a nearby restaurant, Reese told her about the Valeron spread, their town, and the size and numbers of his extended family. It was idle conversation and it helped her to relax. Here was a man who didn't fault her for her past, knowing she had been an innocent victim. He was, as Ella had put it, a very gentlemanly sort.

There were three others waiting at their table. Jared gave her a nod of greeting. Next, Reese introduced the other two – a younger man as his cousin, Shane, and a competent-looking gent and soon-to-be brother-in-law, Landau. Once seated, they proceeded to concern themselves with a good meal, while discussing a number of topics – none of which included their present situation. That was left until after they had finished dessert – the first apple pie Marie had eaten since long before she had been captured.

'Way I see it,' Jared began earnestly, 'if Brett can't get us some kind of extradition for this bunch, it'll be up to us to see that justice is done.'

'You mean *hang 'em all,*' Landau said, showing a semi-serious smirk.

'Killers, kidnappers, slavers, whiskey-peddlers to Indians – hell . . . uh,' he corrected quickly, remembering a lady was present, 'I mean you're durn tootin!'

'The local sheriff is not going to be much help,' Shane put in his own thoughts. 'And I suspect the judge also thinks the Macreedys are simple horse ranchers. We go up against them and we're liable to end up on the wrong side of some wanted posters.'

Jared dismissed his warning. 'I sent a wire to Brett about extradition, but I reckon the gang would have to be arrested and held by the US Marshal's office. After that, the officials from the Canadian government would have to make a formal request – could take weeks or even months.'

'And the only witnesses are a bunch of Indians who were riding there to kill the whiskey dealers, except for the lady here,' Reese pointed out. 'With her being Big Nose's captive squaw, most any jack-leg lawyer could shoot down or even dismiss her testimony.'

'Wouldn't be any complaint if we had to defend ourselves against them,' Shane opined. 'They might try and take Miss Singleton away from us.'

'I doubt they'll be that obliging,' Jared countered. 'Take a look at her – as proper and respectable looking as any woman in town. No one would support those mangy critters trying to make her their slave again. At most, they could ask us to shell out a few bucks to repay whatever they paid for her.'

Landau suddenly smiled. It was so unexpected and unusual, the other three men all stopped thinking or talking, waiting for him to share his idea.

'These men claim they're making an honest living catching, breaking and selling horses. But we know they are brewing whiskey somewhere on their place.'

'So?' Shane was curious. 'What are you suggesting?'

'Our best option might be to prove to the people in this town that the Macreedys are the lowlife, stinking, vermin we know them to be.'

Shane grinned. 'I get it. If they aren't catching and breaking horses, where does their livestock come from?'

Landau nodded. 'And if they aren't using an illegal still to make the fire-water they are trading to the Indians, they can't complain if that still gets put out of operation.'

'Let's give Brett a day or two to see what our lawful options are,' Reese cautioned. 'Be a shame if we started a small-scale war, when Brett might have an answer to our problems.'

Landau conceded to his suggestion. 'OK. We can sit back and wait for a spell, but Scarlet is only going to wait for a week. We need to wrap this up in the next few days. If Brett informs us there isn't a legal way to get these guys, we should have a plan in place to deal with them ourselves.'

'There are seven of them, plus no support from the sheriff and judge,' Marie announced her concerns for the first time. 'I can see you are decent, honorable men, but that still leaves you facing two-to-one odds.'

Jared laughed. 'Missy, our family took on an entire outlaw stronghold of over a hundred men to get our sister back, after she had been kidnapped. When everything was said an' done, we left without losing a man and Landau here became one of our family. . . .' He grinned. 'Well, he will be if he plays his cards right in Denver. So, don't you worry about us. If it comes to a fight, we'll even the odds right quick.'

Reese stood up and moved behind Marie to pull her chair back when she also came to her feet. Then he looked at the three men still at the table.

'You guys decide how you want to handle this. I'm going to see Miss Singleton home and will catch up with you at the hotel.' He paused. 'Who am I sharing a room with?'

'Uh, that would be me,' Landau said.

'Yeah,' Shane taunted, 'you old men share a room and us younger guys share a room.'

'We know you older gents need your sleep,' Jared chimed in.

Reese shook his head. 'Pa never beat you enough, Jer – same goes for Uncle Temple and you, Shane. You're supposed to respect your elders.'

'We do!' Shane showed total innocence. 'We respect your right to privacy and going to bed an hour after sundown.'

Reese gave a nod to Landau and he playfully punched Shane on the arm.

'Ow!' Shane complained, rubbing the spot next to his shoulder.

'Just a reminder from us older men,' Landau said. 'We aren't so old that we can't whip you two!'

It was not yet midnight when Seevy entered the Macreedy home. Quinn and Stewart were sitting at the table playing cards. There was a bottle of store-bought whiskey and a couple glasses in front of them. Both men pushed back from the table at his arrival.

'Didn't expect you till morning,' Stewart greeted him.

'I had to wait until Cotton had time to talk to Donovan. Then it took four drinks and an hour before he gave up what he knew.'

Thinking of the easy-going part-time deputy, Quinn grunted. 'I hope it was worth your time and money.'

Seevy pulled up a chair and sat down. He took the bottle and Stewart's empty glass and poured himself a drink. After downing it in a single swallow, he leaned back and told them what he had learned.

'Took me a while tuh pick out the men who grabbed Washta. We drew a tough hand there, 'cause at least two of them fellers are Valerons.'

He let the news sink in. Stewart groaned and Quinn slapped his forehead with exasperation. Both of them uttered oaths, but waited for Seevy to continue.

'Tell you another thing, Stu, we were completely flim-flammed by that gal. I was keepin' an eye on the one Valeron when he stopped by the Harmon House. A few minutes later, he come out with a finely-dressed, good-lookin' female. I studied on her fer ten minutes before I recognized it was Washta!

'What?' Quinn howled. 'You mean she was dressed as a proper lady?'

'A whole lot more pleasin' tuh the eyes than we give her credit fer,' Seevy claimed. Then he went on with his surveillance. 'The two of them went tuh the restaurant and joined three other men. One of the three looked like he might also be a Valeron – had the same look about him.

Don't know about the fourth man, but he looked like he'd ridden both sides of the river. I wouldn't want tuh face off agin' any one of the four.'

'What did you learn from Cotton?'

'Exactly what we feared. Washta must have told them about the Mounties, cause them boys asked the sheriff tuh arrest us.'

'Donovan knows better than that,' Stewart avowed. 'He's altogether ignorant about our operation.'

'Yeah, he told 'um we had been workin' the past coupla months, roundin' up horses fer an upcomin' sale. The ruse of Porky going in and tellin' his stories each week give us a good alibi. Thing is, with Washta knowin' the truth, the Valerons ain't gonna buy it.'

'What do you think?' Quinn asked his brother.

'Donovan is strictly a city lawman; he won't try to arrest us. And no one can prove we killed that last Mountie. As for the two across the border, even if they knew it was us, ain't no law here can touch us for it.'

'Washta was there, Stu. She knows Eddie and the others opened up on them two Mounties.'

'She was an Indian squaw at the time. Her word won't mean a damn thing.'

'What do you think those fellows will do?'

Stewart rubbed his chin thoughtfully. 'We had best keep an eye on them until we know their plan. If they ride out with Washta, that will likely be the end of it.'

'Cotton said they told the sheriff they were gonna rest their horses fer a coupla days,' Seevy informed them.

'OK,' Stewart replied. 'Then we'll wait them out and see what they do next. If they try and give us any grief, we'll defend ourselves.' He grunted. 'At least, we'll make it look like we were defending ourselves.'

Quinn grinned. 'Yeah, as long as we place their bodies in the yard, we can claim anything we please. Donovan won't investigate it none.'

Stewart looked at Seevy. 'You and Korkle will need to stick close to the house. Eddie can get by with Porky at the still for a day or two. As for Noonan, he can get the load of coal and then take the wagon and barrels up to the still.'

'I'll ride up there tomorrow and tell Eddie what's going on,' Quinn said. 'I can stick around a bit and let him catch a little shut-eye for a few hours – him and Porky both.'

'Good idea. With the still in operation, we need to monitor the brewing real close. Be a big setback if we lost this batch and had to start over.'

'Want me tuh slip back into town?' Seevy asked.

Stewart shook his head. 'They said they were going to rest their horses a day or two. We don't want them getting wise to us being on alert. I'll ride in and have a talk with the sheriff about Washta running away. My concern will only be for her safety, so it won't appear that she was working here against her will.'

'Good thinking, big brother,' Quinn said. 'As far as we know, the gal conked Noonan over the head and simply ran off.'

'That will eliminate any grounds for those Valeron boys to think they have to defend the squaw,' Stewart reasoned. 'If we give them no reason to stay, they might ride on.'

'That would suit me fine,' Seevy agreed. 'I didn't like the looks of them fellers. Nope, didn't like their looks a'tall.'

*

Marie partook of the Harmon breakfast and had chosen a chair on the front porch to enjoy the morning sun. She was pleasantly surprised when Reese arrived a few minutes later. He had taken time to shave, was wearing freshly-laundered clothes, and even his boots were clean and polished. He removed his hat upon entering the Harmon House yard and approached her hesitantly.

'Mr Valeron,' she greeted him warmly. 'I hoped I would see you today.'

'Well, Mrs Harmon pointed out that you couldn't very well get by with a single outfit to wear. I thought we might visit the general store or a dress shop I saw a few doors down from the saloon.'

She rose to her feet and joined him, but did not hide her concern. 'I can't continue to be a burden and expense to you,' she objected. 'You and your brother risked your life for my freedom and a second chance at life. I already owe you more than I can ever repay.'

He laughed, placing his hat over his full head of hair. 'We Valerons are notorious for taking in strays and lending a helping hand. Being blessed by the Lord, we make an effort to aid those less fortunate when we can.'

'How many preachers are in the Valeron family?' she teased.

'Nary a one,' he admitted. 'But Nash is a doctor and Brett is a lawman. That ought to count for something.'

'I need to find a job, a way to pay my own way,' she said. 'I don't wish to impose on other people's generosity.'

Reese turned around and the two of them began to

walk down the main street in town. After a few steps, Reese cast a sidelong look at her.

'If you don't mind my asking, Miss Marie, have you decided on where you want to go?'

Marie felt the pang of being alone and did not return his look. What could she say? Her entire world had ended the day of the Indian raid.

'My family emigrated from England when I was ten years old. My father worked as a teamster until he earned enough money that we could move westward and buy a plot of land. We had 160 acres and had been farming it for two years when the raid occurred.' She shook her head, suffering the grief of the memory. 'My parents and both of my younger brothers were killed outright. I got hit with a war club and didn't wake up until the next day. The braves traded me to a second band of Indians and Big Nose claimed me.'

'How did you end up in Canada?'

'There was a migration of many Indians after a battle at a place called Little Big Horn.'

'Yes,' Reese contributed. 'After a couple hundred soldiers were killed, the army sent several thousand troops to punish the guilty Indians. I remember reading that a great many of them crossed the border to escape retaliation.'

'Big Nose and his band were stragglers, and had avoided the army for a couple years. They traded for me, about the time they decided to go to Canada. Once he took me for his woman, my fate was set.'

'So you spent almost two years in an Indian encampment,' Reese finished her story. 'That must have been a terrible existence.'

'It's something I will never forget, and probably never live down. Being enslaved and degraded – it's very hard to move past what happened to me.'

Reese took her hand. 'My father used to say that no one can change their past or undo their mistakes, but God gives us a fresh chance each and every morning to start anew. I reckon this is your first morning to do just that.'

'But, if I was to relocate and make a place for myself, I can still not hide what happened to me. I mean, a man would have a right to know that I'd been. . . .' She struggled for the right word.

'What?' Reese prompted. 'A victim? An unwilling hostage who was forced to endure what no human should ever have to suffer?'

Marie put a critical look on him. 'You know most people will see me as . . . as soiled or disgraced. How can I pretend to be a lady, when I've been an Indian's squaw?'

Reese did not flinch under her verbal eruption. Instead, he gazed directly into her eyes. 'A person's spirit is more than the body itself, Miss Marie. If your spirit is pure, those who wish to know you will see you in that light. I suggest you consider that hot bath you took yesterday as a cleansing of your body and mind from all of the vile degradation you've suffered. Consider yourself to be as fresh as this wondrous new morning, with a clear blue sky and the sun shining brightly down on us.'

Marie looked at Reese with a measure of disbelief. Here was an ordinary rancher, consoling and lecturing her like a doctor or parson. Truly, there was more to this man than met the eye. He had a rare quality she'd not seen before – insight? Compassion? Discernment? Possibly a combination of all of those traits.

'I want to accept your suggestion and take it to heart,' Marie murmured softly. 'You almost make me believe I can start over.'

'Miss Marie,' Reese displayed a serious mien, 'when I look at you, I see strength, grace and innocence. The true disgrace for a victim comes from pompous, cruel or hard-hearted hypocrites – they are the ones who should be ashamed.'

'Very well, Mr Valeron,' Marie gave in. 'I shall be a new person today, and try to not dwell on the past.'

Reese smiled, and it was as natural on him as wearing a hat. In fact, he was much better-favored than she had first thought – perhaps due to his inner goodness shining through.

CHAPTER SIX

Jared got a reply from Brett, but it didn't offer much assistance. He had sent a wire through the proper channels to the commanding officer at NWMP headquarters in Canada. His contact in the justice department doubted very much if an extradition would be feasible, considering the lack of evidence or witnesses.

Jared passed the word to Landau and Shane, who would tell Reese. Meanwhile, he visited the sheriff again.

'I can put your mind to rest,' Donovan told him right off. 'Stewart Macreedy stopped by this morning. He was worried that someone had kidnapped their housekeeper. I learned from Carl Harmon that you and your brother had brought the lady into town and were seeing to her welfare. Stewart wanted me to thank you for your trouble. Seems a whiskey dealer they knew sold the lady to them a few weeks back. The trader had rescued the woman from a life of servitude in an Indian encampment across the border. That explains the confusion about the Macreedys being involved in anything underhanded.'

'The guy I used my gun butt on was attacking the lady,'

Jared told him.

Donovan waved his hand to dismiss the incident. 'Yes, Stewart told me they warned the man – Noonan is his name – to never touch another woman or they'd fire him. I've had to toss him in a cell a time or two for getting rowdy with the gals who work in the saloon.'

Jared fixed a sour look on the lawman. 'Everything is neat and tidy, wrapped up like an expensive present, with a pretty bright-colored bow. That's about what we expected.'

'Look, Valeron,' the sheriff growled. 'I done my duty! I looked into your claims and got to the bottom of this here story. Ain't no way the Macreedys could have gone to Canada and killed anyone. They have spent the past few months rounding up and breaking horses. They've got a herd ready to sell to prove it!'

'Marie Singleton was there when the Macreedys sold whiskey to the Indians. Big Nose traded her for a jug and she witnessed the killing of two Mounties when they showed up to close down their operation. The Macreedys had taken her and a couple young girls in trade for liquor. Those unfortunate girls were sold up in Montana, but they kept Miss Singleton to do their cooking and cleaning. She told us the trader called Seevy killed a third man who was following after them. He's the dying man we found on the trail – Brock Gordon, recently of the Mounted Police.'

'Yes, yes, you told me most of this story before. But what do you expect from an angry, discarded squaw? It's likely she wants to strike back at anyone connected with her being traded like an unwanted horse.'

Jared took a sudden step forward and grabbed the front

of the sheriff's shirt. He yanked the man up onto his toes and bared his teeth in a snarl.

'You ever call that lady a squaw again, Donovan, and, badge or no badge, I'll knock you into the middle of next week!'

Donovan was too shocked to be indignant. 'W-well . . . sure,' he stammered. 'I didn't mean nothing. It's what Stewart called her – I was only repeating his words.'

Jared let go and stepped away from the lawman. However, he didn't have a change of expression. The helpless ire he felt was knowing the Macreedys were safe from prosecution in this town.

'You know I'm telling you the truth,' he accused Donovan. 'You know it and you don't give a damn. So long as you get paid, and no laws are broken inside the city limits, that's as much as you care to know.'

He bridled at the statement, having collected a measure of composure. 'You have no right to say that to me, Valeron. I don't know for certain that the Macreedys have done one blessed thing wrong.'

'When a man with a badge – whether he be a sheriff or the Attorney General of these United States – refuses to enforce the laws of our land, it's up to the people themselves to do what is right.'

Donovan pointed a warning finger at him. 'Don't put yourself above the law, young man. If you do something rash, you may end up behind bars yourself.'

'I told you before – don't threaten me, not when you're on the wrong side of that badge!'

Donovan held his tongue as Jared left the office. As Jared had suspected from the start, any retribution for the deaths of the three Mounties, and the selling of innocent Indian children, was going to be his family's responsibility.

'The guy stole our housekeeper!' Noonan whined to Stewart. 'He come onto our place, clubbed me from behind and took Washta.'

'I warned you to let her alone!'

'She was teasing me, Stu . . . moving real sexy like and giving me the eye.'

Stewart snorted his disbelief. 'Washta never once looked any of us in the eye. She was about as meek as a field mouse. Besides which, I told you before – the woman is white!'

'Don't make a bit a difference – a squaw's a squaw,' he argued.

'Let it go, Noonan,' Stewart warned him. 'She's out of our lives and out of our reach. I set things right with Donovan. Don't you go messing up our set-up here, or else you'll be looking for a new place to hang your hat.'

'Holy hell, Stu!' he cried. 'The woman was ours! You expect us to sit by and let a couple yahoos get away with trespassing and kidnapping?'

'Our operation is more important than your petty conquests. You best get that through your thick skull.'

Noonan swore, but turned around and left for the barn. He still had one more brace to attach to their new wagon. After that. . . . He sulked as he crossed the yard, a burning rage lingering beneath the surface. Telling himself Washta was white didn't change a thing. He had been one second away from bending her to his will – close enough that he could feel her body against his own, and though she had turned her head, her cheek was soft. Her flesh was warm and yielding. . . .

Noonan forced the fantasies from his head. She had denied him his pleasure, but she was staying in Rimrock, still within reach. He had no access while she was inside the boarding house, but she wouldn't stay there forever. As soon as she felt safe and wished to test her new independence, she would venture out on her own. He only needed a covert window, a slim portal of opportunity, and he could grab her.

Reason threatened to enter his mind, but he took the small flask of whiskey from his pocket and took a swig. Raised on a farm with seven other kids, working from daylight to dark, more slaves than children, he had learned to rely only on himself. The war allowed him an escape and he took advantage of the conflict to fulfill his first conquests. Widows, wives, daughters – so many were left vulnerable during the fighting. And every soldier looked like another – who could identify him among the thousands in the field? After the war, he had turned to robbing and stealing. It was good fortune when he met up with the three Macreedy brothers. Their profession allowed him plenty of money, along with access to Indian maids, wives and widows too. Never knowing about or caring for actual love, he was happy to settle for fulfilling his lustful nature. He didn't want a wife, kids and responsibilities – he enjoyed the chase, the fun, and being able to subjugate a woman and take what he wanted from her. Washta had denied him his conquest, his prize. Well, she would make a mistake, and he would be there to collect the debt.

*

'Well?' Scarlet asked in a rather demanding tone, before Nash had even closed the front door to his doctor's office. 'Did you get a telegraph message from Reese?'

Nash winked at Trina, who was standing alongside his sister. 'Do you think he's the one Scarlet is dying to hear from?'

Trina giggled at his teasing, but Scarlet placed her hands on her hips and tapped her toe impatiently. 'Did you get a wire or not?'

Her exemplary tone allowed Nash no further wiggle room. 'I got a telegram – yes, – but not from Reese. It came from Brett.'

'Brett?' she queried. 'Why is Brett sending his wire to you?'

'Keeping you informed, no doubt,' Nash replied. 'I'm sure he doesn't expect me to personally do anything about the situation over at Rimrock.'

'Nash, dear,' Trina got involved. 'Don't be so mean. You can see your sister is worried sick over this whole thing.'

'Reese has a level head,' Nash retorted easily. 'He won't let the guys get into any trouble they can't handle.'

'You don't know that,' Scarlet maintained. 'Jared is with Reese now, and I gave my promise to a dying man. You know what that means.'

Trina turned her head to frown at Scarlet. 'What does it mean?' she wanted to know. 'Anyone of good conscience would pledge their word to comfort a dying man. I'm sure the Mountie wouldn't expect anyone to go outside the boundaries of our justice system to fulfill a promise.'

Scarlet smiled at Nash's wife, a tolerant simper, as if the poor girl had missed the point of a poignant story. Rather than actually laugh at her ignorance, she took time to explain.

'Growing up, Reese was busy doing the work of a ranch foreman, Brett pinned on a badge, and Nash here was constantly studying medicine. That left Jared to look after me and Wendy. He was several years older than us, but he has always been a very dedicated big brother.

'One time, when I was about fifteen, a young ranch hand I didn't particularly like took a shine to me. He often tried to catch me out alone and hounded after me constantly. I tried to put him off, but one day, he grabbed me and tried to force me to kiss him.' She sighed at the memory. 'I managed to escape his grasp – he didn't wish to hurt me – but that was the last straw. I broke down and told Jared.'

'I remember,' Nash added to the story. 'What was the guy's name – Chad something?'

'Yes, Chad Billingsly. He drew his time and left the ranch the very next day.'

'He was my first broken-nose to deal with,' Nash said. 'I managed to set the bone straight and applied some tape. Didn't much help his two swollen black eyes – those almost always come from a broken nose.'

'Jared warned if he ever saw him again, he would do far more than punch him in the face,' Scarlet reminded him.

Trina smiled. 'It must be nice, having a brother who cares for you. Me and my half-brother never got along at all. He eventually wanted me dead. Either that, or committed to an asylum for the remainder of my life.'

'My point is,' Scarlet got back to their present situation. 'I gave my promise to that dying man. Jared knows I did, and he will do whatever it takes to fulfill my vow.' She let out a purposive breath, 'And I do mean *whatever it takes*!'

'I suppose Jared knows why Landau is escorting you to Denver too?' Trina asked.

Scarlet put a sharp look on Nash. He shrugged and pointed to the ring on his finger.

'Uh, no secrets in our marriage, Sis.'

'It's true,' Scarlet admitted. 'I'm sure Landy is going to ask for my hand. I mentioned one time that I thought it would be romantic to be proposed to at a fancy restaurant, with candlelight and champagne. I'm not supposed to know it, but he ordered a ring from the Valeron general store's catalog. I know for a fact that it arrived a couple weeks ago – coincidentally, about the time Dad suggested I make the trip to Denver.'

'So everyone knows what's going on,' Trina postulated, 'except Landy – as you call him. He still thinks it's a secret.'

Scarlet laughed. 'Yes, that's it exactly.'

Nash did some quick thinking. 'All right, Sis, I'll send a reply to Brett and let him know a little more about the situation. He might get involved, in order to head off any rash act on Jared's part.'

Scarlet reached out and placed her hand on her brother's shoulder. 'Thank you, Nash. I would feel terrible if Jared ended up wanted by the law because he was determined to keep my word to the dying Mountie.'

Nash pivoted about and went back out the door. Trina took hold of Scarlet's hand in a show of support.

'I'm sure the rest of the family will keep Jared from doing anything too foolhardy. I was only around him briefly, but I'm sure he can be reasoned with.'

Scarlet laughed. 'Did Nash tell you about my being kidnapped a year ago?'

'Some. I'm very sorry the man you were going to marry was killed.'

A look of ignominy crossed Scarlet's face. 'He tried to defend me. And it's terrible to admit, but his death made me realize I hadn't actually loved him. When I was taken, I felt mostly fear and dread for myself. It's only now. . . .' She noticeably blushed. 'The way I feel about Landy,' she murmured. 'It's different. You know?'

Trina smiled. 'You've seen Nash and me together. Yes, I know.'

'I felt it was *time* to marry a man then, but I know now what it is to want to marry a man.'

'Many girls marry for convenience or it is arranged by their father. I fear a great many women also marry out of necessity, or the desire to have children and a family. Far too few get to marry because they truly found a man they could love for the rest of their lives.'

Scarlet bobbed her head in agreement. 'Well, getting back to Jared, there were five kidnappers and Landy.' Trina acknowledged Nash had told her about Landau protecting her, so she got to the point of her story. 'Cousin Wyatt killed one of the men in a shootout, and Landy killed the man responsible for taking me during a struggle. The three others – well, Jared hanged them all!'

'But Nash said Brett was there at the time,' Trina recalled. 'You mean he allowed Jared to hang the men without a trial?'

'They were guilty of kidnapping and murder,' Scarlet

replied. 'The punishment in this part of the world for those crimes is hanging.'

'And the punishment for killing those Mounties. . . .'

Trina didn't have to finish. Scarlet simply sighed, 'Uh-huh.'

Reese and Jared remained in town, while Shane and Landau took a ride. Reese described exactly where the Macreedy place was, so they skirted the ranch house far enough to remain unseen. Then they circled around to the mountainous region north of the ranch itself. Off to the east were higher hills, with a grove or two of trees. To the west were rocky canyons, ravines and a stream of water that came from the forested mountains.

'The pastures will be greener on this end,' Shane speculated. 'There looks to be a few places where a short fence could hold a herd of horses.'

'Don't see any riders,' Landau said. 'What's our story if we get caught out here?'

'I'm looking to buy a few mounts for our remuda,' Shane answered. 'And the sheriff claimed they were horse dealers.'

'Just so long as they don't start shooting first – without asking us why we are trespassing about on their land.'

Shane grinned, then proceeded to ride over a couple hills, until they spotted a small herd of horses. There didn't seem to be anyone watching the animals, so they rode a bit closer. Not wanting to spook the herd, they stopped about a hundred yards away.

'My first impression,' Shane spoke up, 'they don't have many horses to sell or trade for a ranch supporting seven men. And I don't see a mustang among them.'

'I count twenty-two head,' Landau agreed. 'And you can make out the brands from here – looks the same marking on every one.'

Shane rose in his stirrups, as if to study them more closely. 'I know that brand. It's a big outfit over in Colorado. We've done a little dealing with them in the past. And you're right, every horse is packing the same brand on its hip. These animals are all from Newton Ingersol's ranch.'

'What do you want to do?'

'Let's get out of here before we're seen. We'll tell Reese what we found and decide our next move.'

Landau didn't dally, but whirled his horse about and they returned the way they'd come, again careful to avoid the ranch house. Once they reached the main road, they relaxed their pace and let their horses walk.

'Time's getting on,' Shane warned Landau. 'What are you going to do if we don't have this settled in the next couple days? Reese said Scarlet told you she was only going to wait a week for you.'

'Durned if I know,' Landau admitted. 'I hate to miss out on this chance. It might be months before I can figure another scheme to get her to a fancy place in a big city.'

'Are you worried she might say no?'

The man shook his head. 'It's been a year since her betrothed was killed, and she confided in me once that she hadn't truly loved the man. She said turning twenty-four got her to worrying she would wait too long and maybe not have time for the three or four kids she wants. Fred Logan was on a successful path and she figured he'd make her a good husband.'

'But the fire wasn't in her blood for him, huh?'

Landau laughed. 'From what she told me about him, I don't think so.'

'What about you?' Shane wanted to know. 'You had a wife once – are you sure you are in love with Scarlet?'

'My wife was a mistake I made when I was about Cliff's age. I thought any gal would prefer marriage over sharing her favors to earn a living. I wanted to give her a chance at a respectable life. Turns out, she didn't enjoy being faithful or respectable.'

'Yeah, Jared told me about your situation.' Landau snorted his acknowledgment, and Shane added: 'You know how close Scarlet and Jared are – she tells him something in confidence and he tells the rest of the world. Not much for keeping secrets, my cousin.'

'Once we're married, I'll try and be her one and only confidant.'

CHAPTER SEVEN

Slick Noonan unloaded the coal at the bin around to the rear of the house. He stopped for lunch with Stewart, Quinn and Korkle. Seevy was due back from town, having been sent to keep an eye on what the Valerons were up to. As soon as he had eaten, Noonan loaded the empty whiskey barrels and headed for the still.

Eddie and Porky were busy stacking wood. They had gathered enough to keep the burner going for several days. Porky would continue to gather and cut more timber while Eddie kept an eye on the brewing.

'Stu said to leave the team,' Noonan relayed to the youngest Macreedy. 'Porky can tether them where they can get the grass up here for a few days. No sense in feeding them hay when this place is covered with greenery. Plus you can stake them so they can reach the water.'

'No sweat, Slick,' Eddie told him. 'There's lots of fodder along the creek bank. You can take Porky's horse back to the ranch.'

Noonan smiled his approval – Eddie was the only one who called him *Slick* all the time. The others were usually too busy calling him more critical names!

'You need anything from town?' he asked Eddie. 'My order of Macassar is due in, so I can pick you up whatever you want.'

Eddie gestured no. 'We're set here for the next few days. You want to do something for us, come back and lend a hand so we catch a few hours extra rest.'

'I'll do that,' Noonan replied. 'Stu was saying he would be sending you some relief again in a day or two anyway.'

Eddie raised a hand in farewell and returned to check the heat gauge on the vat of mash. It appeared everything was working fine.

Noonan left for town, but he wasn't thinking of his hair tonic. He wanted to get a look at Washta, now she had decided to be a white woman again. He hadn't slept worth a hoot since she had eluded his clutches. He needed a way to get her off alone. She could be nice to him, or he would spread her story around town. He was sure she wouldn't appreciate that. If only there was some way to. . . .

An idea formed in his head and he smirked a twisted smile. *Yes . . . that ought to do the trick!*

Shane and Jared were out looking over the country, seeking to find the Macreedy still. As Shane knew where the horses were, he could point it out to Jared. If the time for action came, it would help if he knew the lay of things. As for Reese and Landau, they were playing cards in the lobby of the hotel. The establishment provided a sitting room and provided drinks for their customers, as many of their guests were travelers making connections on the stage. It allowed them a place to socialize or read while passing the time.

'Did you remember to send a telegraph message to Scarlet?' Reese asked Landau, as he studied the cards in his hand. 'There isn't much to do in Castle Point. She's going to get bored real quick.'

Landau tossed out a card and sighed. 'For all the good it will do,' he said. 'Scarlet is nothing if not a woman of her word. The week's gonna be up before we can settle this.'

'She wants to make the trip with us,' Reese replied confidently. 'If she thinks we will be there a day or two late, she will wait. I'm betting she has an inkling as to what you have planned for Denver.'

He looked up from his hand. 'How could she?'

Reese laughed. 'It's not as if your courtship is a big secret. How many times do you think my father has sent her to Denver to pick up a special order?' At Landau's shrug, Reese said: 'Never. Same goes for me. Pa has taken Mom with him, or Uncle Temple or Udal would take their wife. It's a special trip, a rare occasion to enjoy a couple days in the city. Everyone took a pass this time, just so you could take Scarlet.'

Landau skewed his expression. 'You mean everyone on the whole blasted ranch knows my plan?'

'You two have been an item together since returning from Brimstone. A year has passed since Fred Logan was killed – adequate time for Scarlet to move on. Those on the ranch who haven't guessed the reason for our trip have to be pretty dense.'

He grunted. 'So much for a surprise engagement.'

'What's it matter, so long as the chore gets done?'

'Well,' Landau turned the tables, 'speaking of romance

and getting chores done – what are your intentions concerning Miss Singleton?'

Reese sat up straight. 'What?'

'Come on,' Landau said. 'I've seen the way you two look at each other. You are her hero, the man who saved her from a life of servitude and shame.'

'If you recall, it was Jared who saved her from the attack.'

'Jared isn't the one who looked after her and held her hand,' Landau pointed out. 'And he didn't walk her home or see to her every need or comfort. That's been all you, buddy.'

Reese felt a warm flush. 'Yeah, I suppose I have been spending more time with her than the rest of you. But I can't act on her vulnerability or take advantage of her gratitude. That wouldn't be right.'

'Have you taken time to actually look into that woman's eyes? I'm telling you – give her half a chance and she'll fall into your arms!'

Reese was trying to sort out his thoughts and feelings when a young boy – Bobby, the town runner for the telegrapher – came racing into the room. He was out of breath, as if he had been searching all over town.

'Mr Valeron,' he said, approaching their table. 'I thought . . .' he panted, gasping for air. 'I thought you'd want to know about something strange going on.'

'Shoot, Bobby,' Reese said. 'What have you got?'

'A fellow from the Macreedy place . . .' he sucked in a breath. 'Don't know his name.' Another breath. 'He had me deliver a message to that new lady over at the Harmon House.'

'What kind of message?'

Bobby made a face. 'The kind that are supposed to be private. He gave me four-bits to keep my mouth shut.' The boy shook his head. 'But I didn't like the idea – you know?'

'No, I don't know! Tell me!' Reese demanded, suddenly fearful. 'What was the message?'

'It asked for Miss Singleton to meet him back of the livery.' Bobby violently shook his head. 'And he signed your name to the note!'

'Noonan!' Landau exclaimed.

Reese jumped up from the table. 'Get the sheriff!' he rasped hastily to Landau, and he raced from the room.

Landau pulled a silver dollar from his pocket and gave it to Bobby. 'You done the right thing, kid!' he told him. 'Thanks!' Then he was also hurrying from the room.

A rough hand suddenly clamped down over Marie's mouth. Before she could put up a fight, a strong arm was wrapped around her, pinning both of her arms to her sides. Jerked backward, she was dragged towards a nearby drainage-ditch.

The shock of the action, plus being pulled from behind, made it difficult to put up any resistance. She couldn't kick at the man, but she did dig in her heels and sagged heavily downward, forcing her abductor to support her weight. He began grunting with the effort, as a hundred-and-ten pounds of dead weight – more so, by using her heels to compound his chore – had him struggling.

'Fight all you want,' Noonan's harsh voice rasped. 'You're gonna give me what you owe me, Washta!'

The sound of his voice was enough that she renewed her efforts. She couldn't get her hands free, but she was able to dig her fingers into his upper thighs, gripping as tightly as she could, raking her nails and pinching with all her might.

'Ow!' he complained bitterly. 'You feisty little witch! I get you into the draw and I'll teach you some manners!'

Suddenly, changing her tactics, she pulled her legs under her, then shoved backwards with all her might. Noonan had been pulling and tugging. The abrupt change of direction caught him by surprise. He reeled and tried to backpedal, but tripped over his own feet. The two of them landed on the ground, with him underneath Marie.

Hitting the dirt caused him to lose his hold over her mouth. Marie hadn't tried to scream since she was a child, but she managed a decent cry. It rang out in the still afternoon air like a gunshot.

'Hold it!' a man's voice called out.

Noonan panicked. He tried to throw Marie aside, but she turned into his toss, remaining atop him and slowing his getaway. It allowed the man who had shouted time to arrive – it was Reese!

Reese grabbed her under her arms and pulled her off of Noonan. Before the man could get his feet under him, Reese plunged down on to his chest with both knees. It drove the wind from his lungs.

Noonan attempted to raise his hands, but Reese was not in the mood for a passive surrender. He began to hammer the man with both fists, pounding him with punch after punch. He might have continued the severe beating, but the slight pressure of a hand on his shoulder was enough for him to regain his senses. Standing up, he saw that Noonan was unconscious, bleeding, and several lumps and bruises were forming from being soundly pummeled.

'I don't think he's any threat now,' Marie's soft voice reached his ears.

'Dirty, lowdown, disgusting maggot!' Reese exclaimed. 'Good thing you put up a fight. If he'd have gotten you into the wash, I might have been too late.'

The sound of running feet caused Reese to step back from Noonan's body. The sheriff and Landau skidded to a halt next to them. They looked at the man on the ground, both men's chests heaving from their haste. Donovan put a hard look on Reese.

'Appears you dealt out your own brand of justice, Valeron.'

'Mr Noonan tricked me into coming here,' Marie spoke up, before Reese could reply. 'He grabbed me from behind and was dragging me to the wash. He told me he was going to have his way with me! Mr Valeron arrived to stop him.' She glared at the sheriff. 'This is the second time this man has tried to do me serious physical harm. I have to wonder why he isn't in your jail from his first attack!'

The challenge caused the peace officer to back water. 'I . . . I'm only a town sheriff,' he stammered. 'I didn't have the authority to make an arrest for something that happened outside of the city limits.'

'You're a poor excuse for a lawman,' Landau criticized. 'Are you gonna do your job this time, or do we drag this snake to the nearest tree and take care of him the Valeron way?'

Donovan bridled and came erect. 'I got this!' he snapped. 'I'll take him before the judge first thing tomorrow morning. He'll get a hearing, and Franklin will sure enough set a trial date.'

'He's yours,' Reese told the sheriff. 'But, if he gets off with nothing more than a tongue lashing, I'll see your judge is defrocked as quickly as a priest caught in a brothel.'

'I keep telling you, me and the judge take our jobs seriously. This happened here in town – it won't go unpunished.'

Noonan managed to sit up, ducking his head to spit out a mouthful of blood. 'I want a doctor,' he muttered. 'Feels like half my teeth are loose.'

'You're lucky to have any teeth at all, Noonan,' the sheriff scolded him. 'You damn fool – attacking a woman in my town!'

'She's a squaw,' he whined. 'Injun squaws got no rights in Rimrock.'

Donovan snarled, 'Get on your feet or I'll drag you to jail by your precious hair! If I'd been five minutes later, you would be hanging at the end of a noose!'

Reese felt someone touch his arm and looked at Marie. She was inspecting his hands.

'Looks like you've bruised your knuckles,' she murmured. 'Come to the boarding house and soak them in hot water.'

'You go ahead,' Landau said. 'I'll keep an eye out for Jared and Shane.'

Reese went with Marie, amazed at how quickly she had bounced back from the attack. Ella rounded up a pan of hot water and an old towel to clean the blood from his hands, then left them alone. Until he placed his hands in the water, he hadn't realized how hard he had hit Noonan.

'You're lucky you didn't break a knuckle or two,' Marie said, as she began to pat his hands dry. 'You do have some swelling, but it doesn't look too serious.'

'Kind of surprised myself,' Reese admitted. 'When I saw him trying to – well, when you were fighting with him – I kind of lost my head.' He sighed, 'I've never been that angry before in my life.'

Marie looked at him with a rather perplexing, female-type appraisal. 'Have you never had a fight before?'

'I've mixed it up a time or two, but never lost control. I mean, that's the first time I ever wanted to kill a man with my bare hands.'

She had finished with the towel, but continued to hold his hands. 'You have the hands of a rancher, rough from continued use of a rope and branding iron.'

'That's part of my foreman duties, to help with the branding of steers and working the cattle. Cousin Troy oversees the lumber mill; Shane manages the wranglers and horses; Lana – Shane's sister – her husband oversees the farming; and Cousin Martin is the ranch bookkeeper and sometimes lawyer. I believe I told you my brother, Brett, is a town sheriff in Valeron.'

'And Jared?'

'He's the hunter in the family. Best tracker in the country, and only next to Cousin Wyatt when it comes to using a gun.'

'Such a fine, big family you have.'

Reese swallowed hard, trying to muster his courage,

before speaking again. 'We would have no trouble finding a place for you.' At her surprised look, he hurried to add: 'I mean, we have stores to manage. Plus, we hire housekeepers, seamstresses and the like. Not to mention several cooks for the large number of workers.'

She hid her eyes beneath her dark lashes. 'I don't wish to be a burden to anyone.'

'I can't see an attractive and genteel lady like yourself ever being a burden,' Reese said awkwardly. 'You seem a caring and worthwhile person.'

There was a slight tug at the corners of her mouth, as a vague hint of a smile surfaced on her lips. 'You are a gracious soul, Reese Valeron,' she murmured. 'You speak with such assurance, I almost believe your words.'

'Can't fault a man for telling the truth, Miss Singleton.'

Marie lifted her head, her near-ebony-colored eyes bright and lucid. Reese was captured by the look, lost in the depths of the dark, mysterious pools of the woman's gaze.

'You two doing OK in here?' Ella Harmon interrupted, sticking her head around the corner. 'Need anything? I've got some salve if you need it for your hands.'

'We're fine,' Reese replied quickly, unhappy at the intrusion. 'Thank you.'

The moment was lost. Marie withdrew into herself, displaying only a trace of crimson in her cheeks from the momentary lapse of control.

Reese sighed. 'I'd better go see what is going on. If Jared should arrive, he might try and take matters into his own hands.'

'I understand,' Marie said. 'I think I'll lie down for a bit.

I'm sure I have a couple bruises and strained some muscles. Mr Noonan is quite a bit bigger than me.'

Reese chuckled. 'You did yourself proud, little lady. I'm not altogether sure you couldn't have taken him on your own.'

She smiled. 'No . . . I was losing the fight. You didn't arrive one instant too early.'

'See you later.'

Marie tipped her head in a nod. 'You know where to find me.'

The judge owned the barber shop and bakery, and had been a circuit judge for several years. He had an ailing back and could no longer travel, but still sat on the bench for all local matters. Reese learned that he was a temperate man who refrained from drinking and gambling. He had a shock of white hair, permanently mussed as if he had just walked through a small tornado. However, his piercing green eyes glowed with purpose and conviction.

'What do you think?' Jared asked Reese. 'Man looks like he ought to be a fire-and-brimstone parson.'

'Guess we'll find out right quick,' Reese replied, giving a bob of his head towards the back of the town hall.

Sheriff Donovan had shackled Noonan's hands and the chain rattled as they made their way to the front row and stood before the judge.

'Lemme hear the charges, Sheriff,' the magistrate spoke up.

'This man – Slick Noonan – attacked a woman back of the livery, Your Honor,' Donovan declared. 'He sent her a note, pretending to be one of her friends, then grabbed her.'

'Continue,' the judge prompted.

'There can be no doubt he intended to force his attentions upon the woman,' Donovan said. 'The town runner informed the man whose name Noonan used on his note. That man – Reese Valeron – he arrived in time to stop Noonan from doing the lady too much harm.'

The judge gave Noonan a second look. 'Appears he also dealt out a little justice himself.'

'Cracked my jaw and knocked out two of my teeth!' Noonan complained. 'I just wanted to talk to the squaw – talk! That's all I wanted.'

'I didn't ask you to speak, Mr Noonan!' the judge scolded him. 'Hold your tongue until I give you permission.'

Noonan ducked his head, but muttered an oath under his breath.

'Have you any witnesses to call on Noonan's behalf, Sheriff?' the judge asked.

'Stewart Macreedy said he wanted to say something, Your Honor.'

The judge looked over the gathering and picked out Stewart. 'Speak your piece, Mr Macreedy.'

Stewart stood up. 'I only wished to say that Noonan is telling the truth about the woman in question, your Honor. We traded a whiskey dealer for her. She had been a Sioux squaw for quite some time, and we took her on as our housekeeper. A couple days back, she was kidnapped from our place. Noonan wanted to know if it had been her idea to leave or if she was being forced in some way.'

The judge scowled at Stewart. 'You expect me to believe that instead of going to the sheriff or simply approaching the lady and asking her, Mr Noonan tricked her into meeting him? Then he grabs her and tries to carry her off, so he can speak to her in private?' He harrumphed. 'Stewart, you should be ashamed of yourself. I wouldn't float that notion to a six-year-old, let alone a man of my years and experience on the bench.'

Rather than debate the merits of his argument, Stewart shrugged helplessly and sat down.

'Your turn, Mr Noonan. Let's hear your side of the story,' the judge instructed.

'It ain't like I grabbed hold of some white woman, Judge,' he lamented. 'I mean, the gal's an Indian squaw. She don't got no rights in this town.'

'Is that your entire defense?'

'That, and I've already been punished. Look at my face! That there Valeron give me what-fer.'

'Thank you for pointing out the obvious, young man. Hearing you display such grand and insightful rhetoric, I suggest your best defense is to keep silent.'

Noonan looked dumbly at him. 'Huh?'

'Sheriff,' the judge looked back at him. 'How many men beat on Mr Noonan after his failed attack?'

'Just one,' Donovan said. 'I suspect he was a might over-zealous.'

'Where is the proposed victim, the lady who suffered the attack?'

Marie was sitting next to Ella and Carl. She hesitantly stood up. 'That would be me, your Honor.'

He studied her utterly ladylike appearance and shook his head in awe. 'And Mr Noonan would have me think of you as an Indian squaw?'

'I was taken hostage two years ago, when the Indians killed my entire family. A man named Big Nose took me for his wife. He traded me for a jug of whiskey to the Macreedys. I was rescued from their ranch when two Valeron men arrived to save me from Mr Noonan's first attempt to force himself on me.'

The judge frowned. 'First attempt?'

'It was out of my jurisdiction, your Honor,' the sheriff hurried to explain. 'The Valerons brought her here and put her up at the Harmon House.'

'Donovan,' the judge's voice was harsh. 'You should have arrested Mr Noonan for attacking the lady the first time. Even being a town sheriff, there is a law on the books known as a "Citizen's Arrest". This man should have been in jail.'

The sheriff swallowed his guilt. 'Yes, I made an error in judgment, Your Honor.'

'Slick Noonan!' The judge growled his displeasure. 'It is hereby determined that you shall stand trial for assault, with intent to do bodily harm to a young lady.' He scribbled on a pad of paper. 'We will set the trial for next week and you will be lucky to escape a noose.' He pounded the desk with a wooden gavel. 'This hearing is adjourned!'

CHAPTER EIGHT

Stewart, Quinn and Seevy went to the saloon to discuss the situation. Once they were off in a corner by themselves, sharing a bottle between them, the subject grew serious.

'I was watchin' Valeron and that other guy,' Seevy said. 'The other two Valerons were gone by the time I started watchin'. I didn't see Noonan enter town.'

'Damage is done,' Quinn said. 'It's not your fault.'

'If we leave him in the hoosgow, Noonan will start flappin' his jaws like a headless chicken,' Seevy warned. 'That female-molester will do whatever it takes tuh keep shed of goin' tuh prison.'

'We bust him out of jail and we will all be wanted criminals,' Quinn warned. 'What can we do?'

Stewart was considering ideas and not liking the one or two options open to them. Then a third notion surfaced and grew to dominance. He shushed the other two men.

'Let me give this some thought. I might have come up with a workable idea. One thing certain, we can't leave Noonan locked away or he'll start singing our sins like a drunk on Saturday night.'

'I agree,' Seevy said. 'He's gotta be shut up, else we will all be in a fix.'

Reese looked at the telegraph message and felt a bitter disappointment. He met up with the others for a bite to eat. Once they were seated at a table, he brought up the bad news.

'Brett got a follow-up reply from the Mounties,' he told them. 'The scout who was with Brock and his brother left the country. They have no way of contacting him. And Big Nose and his few followers crossed the border and surrendered. They will be moved to a reservation and, in accordance with the proclamation from the War Office, all crimes committed by them are dismissed. Even if we managed to locate Big Nose, there isn't any leverage or reason for him to testify against the Macreedys.'

'So they get away with murder in two countries,' Landau grumbled. 'Sure don't seem right.'

Jared grit his teeth. 'Scarlet made a promise. I aim to see it is kept.'

Reese lifted his hands in a helpless gesture. 'We agree with you, Jer, but how do we manage it?'

'Got to make them mad enough to fight,' Shane opined. 'If we can't do this legal, we need to have them start the fight.'

'I sent the telegraph message to that horse ranch you spoke of,' Reese said. 'We might get some leverage there.'

'And we know where the still is,' Landau offered. 'There's another card we can play.'

'I'm thinking we might first give Noonan a push,' Jared tossed in his ante. 'Facing a long term in prison, he might be willing to talk, if he thinks it would lessen his jail time.'

'I doubt the sheriff will be inclined to co-operate. He doesn't trust us,' Shane said.

'His deputy would possibly give us a few minutes,' Landau suggested. 'He seems a more cordial sort of fellow.'

'Having Noonan testify would be a lot safer than forcing the Macreedys into a fight,' Reese said. 'We'll give that a shot before we start a private war.'

'I'd as soon give the Seevy character a shot between the eyes,' Jared kicked at the idea. 'The judge could go soft on them – and that man deserves to hang.'

'They all deserve to hang,' Landau concurred. 'But, I agree with Reese. Let's try the legal way first.'

Jared knew three of them were in accord, so he acquiesced to the plan. 'When and how do we question Noonan?'

Reese outlined, 'Carl told me the sheriff and Cotton take turns sleeping at the jail when they have a prisoner. Donovan has a wife at home and she doesn't like being alone at nights.'

'The sheriff spent last night with the prisoner,' Shane said. 'So that means Cotton ought to be handling duty this evening.'

'OK, guys,' Reese said. 'Jared and I will head over there right after sundown.'

Nyla Donovan set the small pot roast on the table and hurried to remove her apron. She was fussy that way, always careful of her dress, always clean and neat, ever conscious of a bit of dirt or a smudge on the stove or cupboard. Hugh affectionately called her 'Miss Tidy'. She was a doting wife and the loving mother of their three kids – all of them grown and having moved away now.

They shared a quick prayer and began to eat.

'I spoke to Ella today at the store,' Nyla said, after a few bites. 'She said that horrible Mr Noonan is going to be sentenced to prison for attacking that poor, unfortunate woman, who had been an Indian hostage.'

'His trial will be next week. Franklin won't be lenient with him.'

'Ella said the Valerons were nice boys. Are you sure they don't have a case to present against the Macreedys?'

'Noonan has been the only hiccup for the whole bunch of them,' Hugh replied. 'The Macreedys mind the law, never make trouble, and pay more than their fair share of taxes. But Noonan – he's an alley cat and has been a pain in my neck since they arrived in the valley.'

'What about the murder of that Mountie out on the prairie?'

Huge displayed a genuine sympathy. 'It's an impossible situation, honey. The Valerons claim the dying man told them he had been shot by the half-breed, Seevy – he works with the Macreedys.'

'I've seen him around town,' Nyla said. 'He gives me shivers.'

The sheriff frowned at her. 'He does? You never mentioned it.'

'Well, you know, it's nothing a person can put their finger on, it's more . . . a bad feeling. If you look into his eyes, it's like looking at the eyes of a fish – there's no soul, no human emotion there.'

Hugh laughed. 'I think the wrong person in this household is wearing the badge. Who else gives you the shivers?'

'Well, Stewart Macreedy is one. Maybe his youngest brother too.'

The news caused him to pause. 'I'm trapped by the law I'm supposed to uphold. To my knowledge, the Macreedys have never broken a law. And the money they bring into this town is a blessing for the stores, the saloon, and helps allow me to pay for a part-time deputy.'

'Well, all I know is, that poor woman was held captive by Indians and somehow she wound up as a slave out at the Macreedy ranch. Have you seen her since she arrived? Why, she looks as much a proper lady as any woman in town.'

'Stewart explained how he traded for her freedom.'

'Freedom?' she lamented. 'If she was free, why did she escape the Macreedys and come in with those Valeron boys? Ella said she looked every bit an Indian squaw when she arrived at the rooming house. You can't believe she was actually free to leave their service.'

'Well, they did provide a place for her. Far as I know, she has no relatives.' He shook his head. 'In fact, honey, a good many Indian captives never want to return home. It's too painful for them. They would often prefer their loves ones to believe they had died.'

'I'm only saying – from an Indian master to a white master,' Nyla continued her condemnation. 'Ella told me the poor woman still has bruises and scars from her mistreatment. After the lady washed her hair and brushed it out, she saw her reflection in a mirror and began to weep. The suffering of that unfortunate soul breaks my heart.'

'She's free now,' Hugh said gently. 'No one is going to make a slave of her again.'

'Thanks to the Valerons.'

'Yes, I know,' he said, waving a hand in a helpless gesture. 'But, honey, it makes no difference what I think. Without evidence, my hands are tied. Just today, the Valerons got an answer back from the North West Mounted Police. The Mounties have been searching for witnesses, but they've had no luck. They need proof to extradite anyone for the deaths of two of their men. As for the third Mountie, the Valerons only have the word of a dying man, and that isn't enough to get past the Macreedy alibis. According to Julian Porkenridge, every man-jack of them has been here all winter long working with their horses.'

'Porky is a trained pet,' Nyla criticized. 'He says and does whatever the Macreedys tell him to. Did you speak to Miss Singleton? Did you ask her about the Macreedys and how they ended up with her as their slave?'

Hugh pushed back from the table, his appetite gone. His wife had a strong moral conscience. She did not see any gray lines between right and wrong. Unfortunately, the law had more gray than either black or white. The laws meant to protect the innocent often protected the guilty to a greater degree.

'She came to Rimrock as an Indian squaw,' he finally spoke warily, defensively. 'A lawyer would claim any of her accusations were out of spite for her treatment. I don't think a jury would take her word.'

There it came – the look all women had. God hadn't had to give women a voice, not when they were endowed with a critical stare that could cause a man to shrink from a sturdy oak tree to a pitiful acorn. It was used whenever a line was crossed, a dispute needed settling, or a man refused to do what a woman wanted.

'However,' Hugh grasped for a lifeline, before he drowned in his own helpless ineptitude, 'the Valerons are not giving up, honey. They may come up with some evidence yet. If they do, I'll be right beside them, ready to arrest any of the Macreedys or their men.'

It wasn't what his wife wanted to hear, but it did soften her intense gaze. After a moment, she uttered a sigh. 'You're a good man, Hugh, darling,' she said softly, subtly adding a bit of encouragement. 'I know you'll do what is right . . . and lawful.'

He didn't have time to reply. The sound of a gunshot caused him to spin from the table, call a quick 'Stay inside!' and grab his hat and gun. Then he was racing into the darkness.

It was a bizarre scene at the jail. Cotton held a gun on Jared Valeron; Slick Noonan was dead on the floor of his cell; the back door stood open; and Reese was cussing at Cotton for being a fool!

Donovan took all of this in as he entered the sheriff's office. Cotton turned from the two Valerons, but kept his gun pointed at Jared.

'Reese here coaxed me outside,' Cotton explained to Donovan. 'This fellow, Jared, he went in to talk to Noonan. Then we hear a shot and I come in to see Noonan is dead-er'n a rock – just as you see him. The bullet hit him square in the heart.'

'But I didn't shoot him!' Jared growled. 'And if this fool hadn't stopped me, I might have caught the man who did!'

'Check his gun,' Cotton said. 'It's been fired.'

'Of course it was fired,' Reese took up for Jared. 'He shot at the man who killed Noonan.'

'Tell me what you actually saw,' Donovan instructed his deputy.

'Me and Reese was out front talking, while Jared went inside the jail. Next thing, I hear a shot. When I go into the room, I see Jared headed out the back door. I called at him to stop or I'd shoot.'

'We had no reason to shoot Noonan,' Reese spoke up. 'We wanted him to turn on the Macreedys and help us put them all in jail.'

Donovan checked the loads on Jared's gun. 'One round has been fired.'

'I shot at the guy who killed Noonan,' Jared confirmed. 'But he was too quick. He got away. Before I could give chase out the back and maybe get a decent shot at him, your deputy threatened to put a slug in my back.'

Donovan looked at Cotton. 'Did you hear two shots fired?'

'I did,' Reese volunteered. 'They were less than a second apart. Jared is pretty fast when it comes to getting his gun in play.'

The sheriff stared at Cotton. 'What about you?'

'I dunno, Sheriff,' he said. 'Everything happened so fast. There might have been two shots fired, but they'd have had to be durn close together.'

Donovan turned to Jared. 'Did you get a look at the

man who fired the shot?'

'Being dark, there was nothing more than a shadow. I was looking at Noonan when he was killed. I drew and fired, but the door was already closing.'

Donovan walked back and looked out the door. The rear of the building faced a hillside, meaning a bullet passing through the opening would be impossible to find. As it was too dark to look for prints, the sheriff was in a bad way. He could either arrest Jared or take him at his word. But with no witnesses and no bullet hole in the door or frame. . . .

'I'll have to hold you tonight,' he made his decision. 'We will check around and see if anyone heard two shots. Without someone to verify that part of the story, I'm forced to arrest you for Noonan's murder.'

'This is a load of hogwash!' Reese cried. 'We had no motive to kill that man!'

'He attacked a woman with whom you've been seen holding hands,' Donovan argued. 'Plus, your brother publicly threatened to kill anyone who tried to harm the lady.' He held up his hands to stop further debate. 'I'm only sticking up for you Valerons here. We have to do this proper, or someone might decide to take the law into their own hands.'

'The Macreedys are behind this!' Jared declared. 'They were afraid Noonan would talk to lessen his sentence. Them boys are the ones you ought to be looking at.'

'I intend to do exactly that, young feller, but let's do this right. Tomorrow is Sunday, so the judge won't be able to have a hearing until Monday. Once you're cleared – that's it. Then I can do some investigating and try and find the real killer.'

Reese put his hands on his hips and uttered a sigh of resignation. 'Best do as he says, Jer. We won't let anyone railroad you into a noose.'

Jared entered the empty cell, while Cotton and Reese carried Noonan to the undertaker's house. As soon as the two were alone, the sheriff tried to reassure Jared.

'Someone else must have heard two shots. I only heard the first one, but was shouting at my wife and grabbing my gun and hat. I didn't hear a second shot.'

'Wasn't but about a half-second between the two,' Jared told him. 'Both shots probably sounded like one. I figure the killer is carrying a Colt . . . or another brand of a .45 caliber handgun.'

'Might as well get comfortable, son,' Donovan said. 'There's nothing we can do tonight.'

'The half-breed, Seevy, killed the Mountie we found on the trail,' Jared pointed out. 'Word is, the man can move like a ghost. Well, this bushwhacker was deadly accurate and vanished without even checking his kill. I'd say he's the man you should be looking for.'

'I'll run down his whereabouts first thing in the morning,' the sheriff promised.

'If your deputy hadn't been so quick to stop me, I might have caught him out there tonight. I've done a fair share of hunting and tracking.'

'Yes, I've heard of you . . . and your cousin, Wyatt. You both have reputations for dealing out your own brand of justice.'

'The Macreedys killed two Mounties up in Canada, Sheriff. They killed another one here in Wyoming. They also sold Indian girls to anyone who had a wad of money.

They are the ones who should be sitting in this cell.'

'There isn't sufficient evidence to extradite them, and the Mountie you found could have been mistaken about who ambushed him.'

'I know the law . . . and its limitations when it comes to finding the truth,' Jared avowed. 'When all's said and done, my sister believed the Mountie's dying breath. That's all the proof I need.'

Donovan did not waste any more time arguing. 'Cotton will clean up the blood when he gets back. Don't be giving him a hard time for doing his job.'

'If he'd have done his job, that back door would have been bolted from the inside. Pretty careless of him to leave it unlocked.'

'What can I say, he's a part-time deputy, unable to hold any other job in town. He follows orders and isn't afraid of a fight. I take what I can get.'

CHAPTER NINE

Scarlet was pacing the floor of Nash's waiting area when a man opened the door. She uttered a girlish squeal of delight and ran over to hug her brother.

'Brett!' she cried. 'I've been so worried!'

'We've got time,' he said. 'Jared's hearing isn't until tomorrow.'

Scarlet stepped back. 'How did you get here so fast?'

'I was transporting a prisoner to Cheyenne. Pa had your telegraph message waiting for me when I arrived. I rode most of the night to get here.'

'There is no proof of a second man!' she exclaimed. 'The judge might decide to hold a trial for Jerry.'

'I'll see what we're up against once I have time to talk with Jared and Reese.'

'You're not going without me.'

He grinned. 'Why do you think I'm taking the long route to Rimrock? I didn't want you making that ride by yourself, and I knew you wouldn't keep your nose out of this.'

'Jerry has always been there for me. I won't let him face this alone.'

'You have your things packed?'

'I'll be ready as soon as I put on my traveling outfit.'

Nash and Trina had heard the excitement and entered the room. 'You're going to stop long enough to eat, aren't you?' Nash asked. 'I haven't seen you since the wedding.'

'We've got a few minutes,' Brett answered. 'I figured to rent a carriage.'

'You can take mine. If I need to transport someone home or bring them here, I can borrow one. The livery man owes me for tending to a couple of his horses.'

Brett laughed. 'All that training and you still end up tending to animals.'

'What can I say – the poorer people barter for services. I also have free haircuts with the barber, for lancing a boil and preventing infection. And we get our coal for free – as part of my payment for seeing to the injuries any of the miners suffer.'

'And how is your nurse doing?' he asked, looking at Trina.

'I'm learning all the time,' she answered. 'Nash is such a dear. No matter what mistakes I make, he never loses his temper.'

'Jared got enough temper for the whole family,' Brett replied. 'He isn't foolhardy or explosive, but he riles easier than the rest of the Valerons.'

'You don't think they have a case against him, do you?' Nash wanted to know.

'From what Reese said in his wire, I'd say he has a good chance of being turned loose. There is really no motive for him killing the prisoner, and it's not something Jared would do. Comes to getting justice, he will hang a guilty party, but he's never gunned down an unarmed man.'

Scarlet returned to the room to overhear his remark. 'I made a promise to a dying man, Brett. You know Jared will do whatever it takes to punish the killer.'

'Yes, but Reese said the victim wasn't the man who killed the Mountie.'

'You two sit down at the table,' Trina spoke up. 'I've got eggs and bacon on the counter and will fix you breakfast. You can't ride all day on empty stomachs.'

Stewart and Quinn Macreedy were both haranguing the sheriff, while Jared sat idly in his jail cell and ignored their ranting.

'He'll have his day in court,' Donovan tried to end their verbal outrage. 'It will be up to the judge.'

'Noonan told us the man threatened to kill him, if he ever put a hand on that squaw again,' Stewart growled. 'Well, he came into town simply to ask if she wanted to return to the ranch as a paid housekeeper – and she physically attacked him. Noonan was trying to defend himself when the other Valeron showed up.'

The sheriff shook his head. 'Noonan spent time behind bars for manhandling more than one gal in my town. Don't give me any bunk about him being an innocent victim.'

'OK, so he deserved a couple years in prison,' Quinn spoke up. 'But his getting rough with the squaw sure didn't warrant being killed in cold blood.'

'You can testify before the judge about Jared Valeron

threatening to kill him, but the back door was not locked. Someone could have opened it and fired the shot that killed Noonan.'

'Yeah,' Stewart jeered. 'And it could have been a lightning bolt that flew down and put a .45 caliber slug in his chest too.'

'You can pick up his body at the undertaker's, if you've a mind to bury Noonan out at your ranch,' Donovan put an end to the conversation. 'If not, we will plant him at the town cemetery this afternoon.'

'Don't much matter to him where he's buried,' Quinn said, sarcastically. 'The man's past caring one way or the other.'

'Two o'clock then,' the sheriff said. 'I doubt you'll have to fight a big crowd – Noonan wasn't the best liked man in town.'

'Just so his killer don't go free,' Stewart warned. 'Valeron or no, we won't stand by and let him get away with cold-blooded murder.'

'See you at the funeral,' Donovan told them. 'Don't be late.'

The Macreedy brothers left the office and the sheriff heaved a sigh of relief.

'Them two fellas ought to be on stage, maybe doing Shakespeare or the like,' Jared commented from his cell. 'That was a pretty fair job of acting.'

'You best hope Judge Franklin doesn't buy into their performance.'

'Did you find anyone who heard the second shot?' Jared wanted to know. 'Noise must have carried down the street. Even you were close enough to hear gunfire, and you said you were sitting at the dinner table.'

'Cotton is still asking around. I believe your kin is too.'

'You don't believe I'm guilty, do you?'

The sheriff shrugged. 'What I believe ain't important. It's what the judge ends up believing.'

'It's like we told you from the first – the Macreedys are the ones who are guilty. Noonan would have likely sold them out to cut down his sentence, but he never got the chance. Stewart and the others are the ones who wanted him silenced, not me. We needed him to talk.'

'You can explain it at your hearing. If Franklin can be convinced of your innocence, you'll be a free man. If not . . . well, a trial date will be set. That's when you can really start to worry.'

'I'll worry about my life, but not my soul,' Jared told him. 'I'm not guilty of this crime – and you know it.'

Stewart and Quinn stuck around town, having a beer, then going to the cafe for a bit to eat. All the while, they were discussing a way to sway the judge. If Valeron wasn't charged, they would become the obvious target for investigation.

'We can't have the law snooping around,' Quinn said, keeping his voice down.

Stewart looked around the cafe. He recognized many of the faces, but saw no one they could hire to do the chore they needed. 'If we could just get one man to claim he was near the jail. One good witness could turn this against Valeron.'

'No one is gonna want to lie to the judge, not when it's a Valeron on trial.'

Stewart did some thinking. 'OK, so we can't make a case against Jared. We have our backs to a wall here. The Valerons will never let this go, not with Washta telling them exactly what we've done.'

'You think a jury would take her word?' Quinn displayed a worried mien. 'I mean, she was an Indian captive for a coupla years. Being bitter and hateful toward us, considering the way we got her, then forcing her to do our housekeeping and cooking – would you take her word for anything?'

'When it comes to her word, it isn't the law that matters. The Valerons believe her and they won't quit until they balance the scales of justice.'

'Damn, Stu!' Quinn complained. 'We're neck deep in a bog and sinking fast. There must be some way we can turn this around.'

The elder brother turned over ideas in his head. To kill the Valerons would only bring more of their kin. They were relentless . . . and vindictive. They could pack up and move, ride a few hundred miles and start over, but the Valerons would keep looking until they found them. If only the woman didn't know. . . .

'There might be a way,' Stewart said, still mulling the notion. 'If I could get a few moments with Washta, we could get out of this mess.'

'She don't want nothing to do with us, Stu. You seen the reception Noonan got.'

'That moron tried to lay hands on her again – he got what he deserved. I told him to steer clear of her.'

'All right, so you make a formal request and maybe get a few minutes with her. What good does it do?'

Stewart allowed a sly simper to cross his lips. 'Trust me, Quinn. I've an idea that will take care of everything.'

As it turned out, Scarlet and Brett arrived a few hours before the hearing was to begin. The two of them met up with Reese, Shane and Landau. Reese explained to Brett that Judge Franklin would listen to the evidence during the hearing and decide if a trial would be forthcoming.

Scarlet and Landau embraced shortly, then took a few moments to be alone. Afterwards, she and Brett proceeded to visit Jared at the jail.

Donovan allowed them privacy by waiting outside his office. Scarlet went to the cell and put her arms through the bars, able to give Jared a hug. The tears misted her eyes as she stepped back to look at him.

'We know you didn't do this,' she said. 'If it was the promise I made. . . .'

'It's all right,' Jared assured her in his usual big-brother fashion. 'The judge is an honest man.'

'How did you manage to get in this mess?' Brett asked, moving to stand next to Scarlet.

Jared explained the chain of events that led to his being incarcerated. He ended by telling them about not being able to find anyone who had heard a second shot.

'But you had no motive,' Brett insisted. 'What good would killing that man have done?'

'He was killed to silence him,' Jared replied. 'It's the only thing that makes sense.'

'What if they hold you over for trial?' Brett asked. 'Is there a weak link in this Macreedy gang?'

'We are waiting for news about their horse herd. It

might be an angle worth pursuing. If not?' He lifted a single eyebrow with uncertainty.

'We won't let them pin a murder on you,' Scarlet vowed. 'If we have to get Father involved and call in Wyatt, every man on the ranch and the governor himself – we are here for you!'

Jared grinned. 'How about that, Brett? Our little sister is going to take care of me. Seems kind of backwards.'

'If we need a good lawyer, Nash knows a couple who work out of Denver.'

'How were he and Trina doing?' Jared asked Scarlet. 'They still acting like a couple of doves at the first sign of spring?'

His sister laughed. Jared had a way about him, so full of confidence that it seemed he was behind bars as a practical joke.

'Yes,' she answered. 'It's rather embarrassing to be around them at times. They get to gazing into one another's eyes and everything else disappears. I felt as out of place as a lamb at a rodeo.'

'Speaking of the way two people look at each other, have you met Marie yet?' Jared asked her.

'No. Reese said she wanted to do some personal shopping. But there was a distinct gleam in his eye when he spoke of her.'

'Never thought it would happen, Sis – Reese hitching up the matrimonial wagon – but it's looking that way.'

'Good for Reese. He's been a bachelor long enough.'

'How about you and Landau?' Jared turned the subject to her. 'Is your trip still on for Denver?'

'Not until this is settled. You got involved in this

because of me. I can't get back to a normal life until you are walking free again.'

'The sheriff and his deputy are coming in,' Brett said. 'Looks like we barely made it here in time for your hearing.'

'Be glad to get it over with,' Jared said, his teeth clenched. 'Soon as I'm out, we'll set to tracking down the party responsible. We've toyed around with these characters long enough.'

The courthouse was full when the judge took his place on a platform, sitting behind a large, elevated desk. The testimony box was nothing but a straight-back chair stationed at the left side of the desk. It also sat on the raised section, a step above the rest of the floor. It was quite an official-looking room for a town of Rimrock's size.

There were several chairs and a couple of tables situated facing the judge – places for the prosecution and defense, along with the sheriff – with six pews for the audience and a special section for a jury. Donovan sat next to Jared, but there was no formal attorney or jury present. With this being a hearing, the judge would call upon people to testify and make the decision as to whether a trial was necessary.

A clerk seated at a small desk off to one side rose to his feet and called: 'Quiet in the court! Judge Franklin presiding.' Then he sat down and took up a notepad and pencil.

'This here session was to have been a formal trial for Buford "Slick" Noonan,' Franklin began. 'Due to his unexpected departure from our midst, we are here today to determine if Jared Valeron is to be held over for trial in the matter of Noonan's demise.'

Franklin glanced at a sheet of paper on his desk, before fixing his gaze on Jared. 'We will hear from the witnesses, then allow you to have your say.'

At Jared's nod of understanding, the judge called on Deputy Cotton to relate the chronological events of the night Noonan was shot. Next, he questioned Sheriff Donovan about his findings. Those being the only two witnesses, other than for Reese. Being brothers, his testimony did not carry much weight. He ordered Jared to tell his side of the story. When finished, the judge pondered the facts for a few moments.

'Was there no one else who heard more than one shot fired?' he asked the general court. He swept his gaze over the people gathered, but no one offered a word. Then he frowned at Jared.

'Son, we have only your word that you fired at an unknown assailant. Can you give me any reason as to why no one else heard the second shot?'

'I'm pretty handy with a gun,' Jared told him. 'I fired in less than a second at the fleeting shadow outside the door. Being as I was inside the jail, I suspect the gunshot sounded more like an echo of the first and did not carry very far.'

'Two shots, fired very close together, could sound like one, Judge,' Donovan offered his opinion from his chair.

Franklin rubbed his brow, obviously not wanting this to go to trial, yet he was bound by law. 'Without someone backing this young man's story, I am obligated to. . . .'

'Your Honor?' a feminine voice broke the strained silence.

Franklin discovered Marie Singleton had rose to her feet. He gave her a professional smile. 'Did you have something to add to this hearing, Miss Singleton?'

Marie took a deep breath and then spoke softly, but very clearly. 'Mr Valeron is innocent, Your Honor. I'm the one who shot and killed Slick Noonan!'

CHAPTER TEN

The first reaction in the room full of spectators to Marie's confession was a stunned silence. Then the place exploded with questions and raised, incredulous voices. The ado grew so loud Judge Franklin had to bang his gavel a full minute to quiet the crowd.

'Please come forward, Miss Singleton,' the judge ordered, once calm had been restored. 'And take a seat in the witness chair.'

Marie ducked her head, the crimson of shame coloring her cheeks. She left a totally dumbfounded Reese with his mouth still open. The shock was equally spread across the faces of nearly every observer in the room. Once seated in the chair, the judge bade her take her time and tell her story in her own words.

'Many of you in this room are aware of my situation,' she began. 'My entire family was slaughtered in an Indian raid and I was taken hostage. A lowly chief named Big Nose took me as his woman and I served him for almost two years. He traded me for a jug of whiskey and I ended up with the Macreedys. They brought me here as their housekeeper and I worked for them a short while, until Slick Noonan attacked me the first time.'

She paused to moisten her lips. There wasn't a whisper passed in the room. She had every person's undivided attention.

'Jared Valeron rescued me from a dreadful fate at Mr Noonan's hands and I was brought to town. I hoped to get back my life, but Mr Noonan used a fake note to get me alone. He attacked me a second time, but Reese Valeron arrived in time to stop him from tearing off my clothes.' She swallowed hard and grimaced at the memory.

'But he was locked up,' Judge Franklin spoke gently. 'He would have been sent to prison.'

'Would he?' she asked cynically. 'For attacking an ex-Indian squaw? And for how long?' Marie shook her head. 'That horrible, disgusting man – he tormented me, he terrified me. He tired to take me by force twice and swore he would keep coming until he got what he wanted. I knew about the last Indian woman he attacked. When she fought back, he killed her!' She swallowed against the lump in her throat. 'I know he would have found a way to get to me, Your Honor. Even if you sentenced him to a year or two in prison, he would have come back. He would have. . . .' But she began to sob, covering her face with her hands.

'Uh, Judge Franklin,' Stewart Macreedy spoke up, drawing attention to himself.

'Speak up, Stewart. Do you have something to add?'

'As the lady has made her confession, I reckon I ought to do the same.'

'Go on.'

'Our horse ranch did rather poorly last year,' he began. 'Being unable to pay our mortgage, we got together a few barrels of whiskey and took them across the border into Canada. I admit we sold the stuff to the Indians, and that's how Miss Singleton come to be working for us.' He raised his hands, palms outward. 'Mind you! We didn't know the lady was white. She looked like just every other abused, overworked Indian squaw.'

'Continue,' Franklin encouraged.

'Come the day we left, a couple Mounties showed up. Noonan lost his head and started shooting. Before we could stop him, he had shot them both, and one of our own men was mortally wounded. We lit out ahead of Big Nose and his band. They had gotten a couple of bad jugs of liquor and were gonna kill us and take what whiskey we had left. We don't know what they did with the Mounties and the man we had to leave behind.'

Stewart showed a deep remorse for the loss of those men. 'We were on our way home, having lost most of our supplies and wagons, when Seevy caught sight of someone on our trail. He and Noonan set up to catch the guy and see what he wanted.' Another sigh of regret. 'Durned if Noonan didn't open fire and kill him. He saw the man was wearing a partial uniform of the Mounties and took the shot before Seevy could stop him.'

Stewart turned his attention to Marie. 'As for this lady, Noonan did kill an Indian woman when she tried to defend her honor, one time. And, in spite of my order that Washta – uh, Miss Singleton – be left alone, he bragged that he intended to make her his woman. Those of you who knew the man, know he was the worst scum of the earth when it came to his treatment of women. If we hadn't needed him for his blacksmithing skill, we would have sent him packing the first time he got out of line.'

'So Noonan is responsible for the deaths of an Indian woman, three Mounties, and two attacks on Miss Singleton.' Franklin made the statement. 'And you, young lady,' he directed his words at Marie. 'You were afraid he would make good his threat and attack you a third time.'

'I-I couldn't sleep soundly a single night while with the Macreedys, afraid he would come to my bed.' She sniffed back her tears. 'And he was so vulgar, so terribly determined, I knew I would never be safe. I'm sorry, Mr Valeron,' she said, looking at Jared. 'I never thought they would blame you. I didn't want you in jail, not when you saved me from Noonan, out at the ranch.'

Her words again caused the hum of the crowd to grow. Most everyone seemed to be supporting Marie Singleton's actions.

Judge Franklin tapped his gavel lightly, just enough to take back the room. 'By the power of this court, I dismiss all charges against Jared Valeron. And . . .' he kept the room controlled, '. . . I believe Miss Singleton acted out of fear for her safety and her very life. There will be no charges brought against her for the death of Slick Noonan.'

Quinn, Korkle and Seevy toasted Stewart, as they celebrated in the sitting room of their modest ranch house. There was laughter and a feeling of relief in the air.

'No more worries about that dead Mountie,' Seevy said. 'The Judge done took every word you spoke as gospel.'

'The Valerons have no reason to stick around,' Quinn added. 'Noonan's death has set us all free and clear. Ain't no law gonna touch us over selling whiskey to Indians in Canada!'

'Eddie and Porky can keep the still running,' Stewart agreed. 'We'll soon have enough to make another trip. We should be able to get there and back ahead of the snows.'

'Sure wouldn't want to be caught in a big storm,' Quinn put in. 'Let's get it done as soon as possible.'

'I'm still sayin' you got a way of sweet-talkin', Stu,' Seevy praised. 'Washta's story was 'bout as good as anyone I ever seen in court.'

Quinn chuckled 'Just goes to show you – there's nary a woman alive who ain't a good liar.'

Stewart grinned. 'Explains how Ma could claim she favored Eddie.'

All four men laughed and then shared another round.

Korkle, who hadn't said a word – he was a taciturn sort anyway – lifted his glass. 'To getting back to business as usual,' he raised the toast. 'This guard duty is ruining my sleep.'

'Spend the night catching up,' Stewart told him. 'Tomorrow you ride out and spell Eddie. He is due a night on the town.'

'How about Porky?'

'He wouldn't know what to do with a woman if she sat on his lap,' Quinn replied. 'Even so, when Eddie gets back out there, you can give Porky a day off.'

Korkle gave a bob of his head.

'You think the Valerons will pull out?' Quinn asked his brother.

'Nothing to keep them here now.'

'Unless they didn't believe the part about Noonan killin' the Mountie here in Wyoming,' Seevy cautioned. 'Could be, they'll figure I had a hand in that.'

'Better keep a sharp eye until they pack their bags and scoot,' Stewart warned. 'We don't want any surprises. Maybe you ought to mosey back into town and check on them. The stage is running to Cheyenne tomorrow. With any luck, some of them will leave on it.'

'They have at least one buggy at the livery too. That latest Valeron and his sister arrived in it.'

'No need for them to stick around,' Quinn remarked. 'There's no proof against us for anything illegal in this country.'

Stewart grunted. 'Let's hope they see it that way. I'm sick to death of the Valerons.'

Scarlet and Marie went to her boarding house room, while the men held a war council. Not one of them believed Marie had shot Noonan. However, she didn't admit the reasoning behind her confession until Reese arrived a short while later. Then the three of them – Reese on the only chair and the two ladies sitting on the bed – got down to a serious talk.

'Let's hear it,' Reese prodded Marie. 'You weren't shopping earlier; you met with Macreedy.'

She didn't deny it. 'He made the offer. He said I could save your life and maybe several other lives too. I'm afraid if you try to take down Macreedy and his men, one or more of you will end up shot or even killed. This was a way to save Jared and stop any potential bloodshed.'

'What if the Judge had thought to have you swear on the Bible?' Scarlet asked. 'He didn't, due to the way you offered up your admission without any coaxing.'

'I was counting on the surprise,' she admitted.

'Is it possible that Noonan did kill all three Mounties – I mean, him and the one hired man who also died in Canada?'

'No to both,' she replied. 'Noonan was with Stewart when the shooting started at the whiskey-trading camp. Neither of them fired a shot before it was all over. As for the one following us, Seevy is the only one who went to ambush him. Noonan was riding next to me. Seevy left and then caught up with us a while later. I heard him telling Stewart they didn't have to worry about the Mountie. He'd left him to die.'

'Shane got a reply from the horse ranch in Colorado. They lost about twenty-five head of horses to several rustlers last year. They lost their trail when a rain storm washed away the tracks. All of the animals were branded.'

'So?' Scarlet asked, unaware of the Macreedy herd.

'So we figure those horses are the ones Shane and Landau found on the Macreedy ranch. Horse rustling is a prison offense. And with your testimony, we can still pin the murders on those men.'

'The sheriff told you he wouldn't arrest anyone outside of the city limits,' Marie reminded him.

Reese displayed a sly grin. 'Yes, but Brett still carries the authority of a United States marshal. He can arrest anyone, anywhere.'

'But. . . .' Marie's expression showed her very real fear. 'But, Reese,' her voice quaked timorously. 'I couldn't stand the pain if you or your kin were hurt or killed. I'd rather go back to Big Nose than take that risk.'

Scarlet slipped an arm around Marie's shoulders in a big-sister sort of way. 'Tsk, tsk,' she soothed her worries. 'My brothers and Landy are not a bunch of untested vigilantes. They came to rescue me when I was being held prisoner in a bandit stronghold. They had to deal with over a hundred men – many of them killers and some of the worst outlaws in the country. Not one of them got a scratch – other than Landy, and he wasn't working with my kinfolk at the time.' She pulled the woman close and hugged her shortly. 'You don't have to worry about them. My brothers know what they're doing.'

Marie leaned back and shyly looked at Scarlet. 'Until this moment, I didn't know how much I missed having a sister growing up.'

Scarlet laughed. 'If you'd have had a sister like mine, Wendy, you may have had a different opinion. I can tell you, little sisters can be a pain.'

Reese laughed along with them, then grew serious. 'All right, so we are going to put a plan into place,' he warned Marie. 'The only requirement for you two ladies is to keep out of harm's way. If everything works out, we will fulfill Scarlet's promise to that dying Mountie and arrest every man in the Macreedy bunch.'

'And if everything goes south?' Marie asked, still anxious.

Reese grunted. 'Then we turn Jared loose with a rope, and justice will be done all the same.'

Seevy entered the house as Quinn was setting a kettle of

stew on the table. Stewart looked up and did not hide his surprise.

'Didn't expect you back tonight,' Stewart greeted him. 'Something the matter?'

'I know it sure ain't for my cooking,' Quinn added.

'There's somethin' in the wind,' Seevy warned them both. 'I didn't see no signs of any of them Valeron people pullin' out. Washta and the new Valeron gal weren't about, but that new feller – I asked Cotton 'bout him.' He narrowed his gaze with a deep concern. 'That there is Brett Valeron – he's an ex-US Marshal.'

Stewart leaned back in his chair, not bothering to fill his bowl with stew. This didn't bode well and he couldn't hide his vexation over the news. 'Damn!' he muttered. 'Damn! Damn! Damn!'

'They might have been hashing out what they were going to do with Washta,' Quinn offered hopefully. 'After all, the boys are all related, other than that Landau character.'

'Did you overhear anything?' Stewart queried.

'Didn't want them seein' me,' Seevy replied. 'One of them was missin' – the feller who's taken up with Washta – and the others sat in the cafe for a couple hours. They did some jokin' and laughin', but most of the time, they looked right serious.'

'What can they do?' Quinn asked. 'Stu cleared up everything at the hearing.'

Stewart muttered, 'Yeah, but Washta knows Noonan didn't kill those Mounties. I coached her on what she needed to say. She followed my directions perfectly, but she knows the truth. If she talks, we could still have trouble ahead.'

'This isn't good,' Quinn spoke the obvious. 'We lost one man in Canada and are down a second man without Noonan. With them boys adding an ex-lawman to their number, the odds are even.'

'I 'spect Landau and Jared Valeron were the two we had tuh worry about before,' Seevy made the accounting. 'But Brett has been under the gun a good many times and proved himself capable.'

'I agree,' Stewart said. 'That Reese fellow and the youngest Valeron are the only two who look more cattlemen than gunmen.'

'We don't know anything for sure,' Quinn held out a hopeful note. 'Come tomorrow, one or more of them might leave town.'

'That's true enough,' Stewart concurred. 'Seevy, you be in town when the stage leaves, and check on Washta and that new lady, the one who arrived with Brett Valeron. See if anyone pulls out. I can't believe they would risk a war while they still have a couple women in town.'

'And if none of them pull out?' Seevy wanted to know.

'You stick around and see if you can overhear anything or decipher whatever plan the Valerons might come up with. We'll all stick close to the house for the time being. I don't want anyone being exposed and vulnerable by themselves. Once we know what the Valerons are gonna do, we'll do some planning of our own.'

Donovan was surprised to see the man at the door, but he opened it and allowed him to enter the house.

The gent barely removed his hat before Mrs Donovan asked if he would like coffee or lemonade. Before he could answer, the sheriff introduced his wife and himself.

'Brett Valeron,' the visitor said in return. 'And some lemonade would be very nice. I'm not much of a coffee drinker.'

Brett sat down on their living room sofa, taking note that a rocking chair was next to the fireplace and a stuffed lounging chair was next to it. He smiled inwardly thinking of the pair sitting in front of the fire and reminiscing about their kids or the sheriff's day at work. He waited for the glass of refreshment and took a sip, finding it only slightly tart and very good. He complimented the lady on her preparation and waited until both of the Donovans were seated.

'I'm told you have three grown children,' he began.

'Two girls and a boy,' Nyla was the one to confirm his information. 'The girls are both living in Colorado, while our son is in Cheyenne. He runs his father-in-law's hardware store.'

'That's close enough to visit from time to time,' Brett said.

The woman frowned. 'They have two children – ages two and six months – and we've not seen them yet. Our boy can't leave the business to visit here, and Hugh can never take more than one day off at a time.'

Brett nodded his agreement. 'Yes, I've met a lot of lawmen, and they seldom get time for any holidays.'

'Speaking of visits,' the sheriff said, 'What's the point of this visit?'

Brett told him what he had in mind. It took some time and effort, but Hugh – constantly pressed by his wife's wishes – was finally swayed. The two men shook hands and Brett left the Donovan house.

As Brett was a lawman, Reese and the other three didn't include him in their meeting that night. They shared a table at the saloon and each had a beer. Sitting next to the wall in a corner, it was also next to a window. That way they could keep an eye outside on the street while discussing the plan they had in mind. After a little small talk, they got down to business.

'Did you send the wire to Valeron?' Jared asked Reese.

'It's taken care of,' Reese replied. 'Takoda and Chayton should be here in time.' At Jared's nod of approval, he asked Landau: 'And you checked on the still?'

'Fires are burning twenty-four hours a day,' he replied. 'They've got enough mash to brew a half-dozen barrels. And the barrels are ready and waiting, along with a converted freight wagon at their camp. They are cooking mash like there's no tomorrow.'

'There's no law against them selling whiskey to the Indians in Canada,' Shane pointed out. 'How can we destroy their equipment without getting tossed in jail?'

'What can they do?' Reese replied. 'They are breaking the law. All alcohol is subject to a Federal government excise tax. We can smash and burn everything at their whiskey-brewing site and they can't do a thing.'

'Sounds like a good time!' Shane was enthusiastic. 'Any idea how to destroy copper? I mean, that's what they use, isn't it?'

Landau spoke up. 'We can melt the tubing and crush the copper vat or tub. By the time we finish, they won't have enough equipment left to give a grasshopper a hangover.'

Reese clapped his hands. 'This will show them! Marie admitted that Noonan didn't have anything to do with the killing of the Mountie we found. We will get even with those killers – even if the law won't touch them.'

'When do we hit the still?' Landau asked.

'Soon as it's dark tomorrow night. They have to figure the tall tale Macreedy gave the judge cleared them of any guilt. They won't be expecting a visit from us.'

'If we're going to have a long night tomorrow, we'd better hit the bunks early tonight,' Shane spoke up. 'I want to be fresh for the fun we'll have smashing that moonshine site.'

'I'll go along with that,' Jared said. 'Let's call it a night.'

CHAPTER ELEVEN

Stewart was red-eyed from being awakened at midnight. He had drunk more than his usual glass or two of legal alcohol. Seeing Seevy at his bedroom door was not a vision he relished – it couldn't be good news.

'Spill it,' he ordered, still groggy and not fully awake.

'Trouble be at our doorstep, Stu,' Seevy told him anxiously. 'Them Valerons are comin' tuh wreck our still.'

'What?'

'I slipped in close enough to overhear them makin' their plans. They know where the still be, and they're comin' tonight.' He frowned. 'Unless it's still *tonight* – kind of lost track of time. Anyhow, they's comin' fer to crash our operation just after dusk!'

'How the devil do they know where our still is located?'

'That there Jared Valeron – he be a powerful good tracker and hunter – so I've heard. Plus, them boys was doing a lot of snoopin' around when they first showed up.'

'All right,' Stewart said, the fog having lifted from his thinking process. 'Come daylight, we'll get busy on a way to stop the Valerons. If it means killing each and every one, that's what we'll do.'

'You know what the story is 'bout them, how they avenge any attack again' their kin.'

'We have a right to defend our property, Seevy. We'll set up such a deadly ambush that not one of them will escape. The only word that will reach the Valeron clan is that this bunch of troublemakers attacked the wrong people. The law will be on our side.'

'So long as it don't get out that we were protecting an illegal still.'

'Our *property*,' Stewart repeated sternly. 'We'll bring their bodies here and place them in the yard. Donovan can't say a word about us defending the house from an attack.'

'Yeah. That ought tuh do the trick.'

'Tomorrow, we'll check on the herd – push them deeper into the box canyon if need be – and then ride over and prepare for our unwanted guests.'

'Wish we had a couple more guns. There will be four or five of them.'

Stewart agreed. 'Yeah, but we can do it. Quinn, Korkle and both of us are good shots. Eddie can make some noise too.'

'What about Porky?'

'We'll send him back here to keep an eye on things. If they ride past, he can have a fire going and make it look like two or three of us are at the house. It'll make them that much more unaware.'

Seevy agreed with the plan and then spun from the doorway. He was a man who could get by on a couple hours sleep and be fresh the next day. Stewart watched him go with some envy. He knew that, even with extra booze in his system, he would lay awake the rest of the night planning and worrying.

It was a big and dangerous step to take on the Valerons, but they were the ones doing the pushing. He and his group had killed several people and a lawman or two during the past few years. They would handle this chore with the same ease and efficiency.

Bolstering his own confidence about the upcoming fight would do little to help him sleep. He had heard of the Valeron code. He hoped it wouldn't apply to a situation like this. After all, the Valerons were the aggressors; they were the ones pushing for a fight. Once they were all dead, it would be deemed their own fault. He could hope their family accepted the outcome without seeking revenge.

Even as the thought entered his head, he knew the best move would be to leave the country and start over some place else. In fact, once the deadly chore was done, they would take their whiskey and herd of horses and do just that.

Scarlet spent the morning with Marie and the pair of them met up with Landau and Reese for an afternoon meal. The men would be leaving at sundown and there were preparations to be made. The deep concerns invaded the festive mood, but Reese was optimistic their plan would work.

'After this is over,' Scarlet spoke up. 'The four of us will go to Denver. While you men take care of the business end of things, Marie and I are going to do some shopping.'

Marie's eyes broadened with surprise. 'Scarlet!' she exclaimed. 'I'm not . . . I mean, I haven't been asked to. . . .' She floundered for words.

Scarlet scowled at Reese. 'You mean, all this time, and you haven't asked her to come to the ranch?'

'Well, Sis, I was. . . .'

'What's the matter with you?' she scolded him like an ill-behaving child. 'You've been gawking and shuffling around like a school boy with his first crush. Now be a man and tell her you want her to come with us!'

'I was getting to it,' he excused his lack of planning. 'I didn't want Marie thinking I expected something in return for helping to rescue her from the Macreedys.'

'For heaven's sake!' Scarlet showed her exasperation. Then she turned on Marie like a prosecuting attorney. 'You think the world of my brother – isn't that right?'

Marie gulped at her candid statement, but gave a timid bob of her head.

'And you . . .' Scarlet rotated about to pin Reese with a domineering stare. 'You will never find another lady as sweet and attractive as Marie. Isn't that right?'

'Well, yeah,' Reese managed weakly. 'She's a better woman than I ever hoped to meet.'

'So!' Scarlet declared. 'Will you two please get aboard the same wagon, so we can get on with planning our trip to Denver!'

Reese cast a sidelong glance at Landau, who had kept his mouth shut and – with considerable effort – refrained from laughing through the short ordeal. 'Do you see the girl you're courting?' Reese asked, battling his own embarrassment. 'Are you ready to take on a range boss like her?'

'There's a simple strategy to handling a woman like your sister, Reese,' Landau said. 'You do what she wants, when she wants, and you agree with her on most everything that doesn't involve her personal safety. If you live within those rules, then you only have to learn that all of the other rules can change from one minute to the next.'

Reese took a deep breath and looked over at Marie. 'I've been meaning to ask you, Miss Singleton. How would you feel about coming home with us?'

Marie managed a tight smile. 'As long as there is no pressure to give my answer . . . I'd like that.'

'There!' Scarlet proclaimed to Reese. 'It's settled. You and Landy only have to keep from getting killed during the next day or two, while Marie and I will decide what we are going to shop for in Denver. After all, she has to start from scratch.'

'I think we're liable to need a freight wagon for the return ride home,' Landau said with a smirk.

It had been dark for two hours and still the Valerons had not shown up. Stewart moved from his position to stand next to Quinn.

'Something is wrong. Seevy said those fellows were fixing to hit us at dusk.'

'Maybe they were talking about tomorrow night?'

'No, he was certain it was this evening.'

'If so, then where. . . .' But he stopped talking as a lone rider appeared down the trail. He was moving pretty fast for it being full dark.

'Don't shoot!' the rider called out. 'It's me! It's Porky!'

The others came from their hiding places as the hired

hand pulled his mount to a stop. He jumped down and began to practically babble.

'They come past the house! Just like you said!' he blurted to Stewart. 'But they went the wrong way. I got my horse and followed after them. They done went after our herd. They took every one of them. They stole all of our horses!'

'What?!' Stewart bellowed. 'They stole the herd?'

'I come as fast as I could, but they are moving them through the dark right now. I don't know where they went. I come to tell you first thing.'

'Seevy!' Stewart roared.

The man was standing not five feet away. He lifted both hands in a helpless gesture. 'They must have figured we'd be watchin' and listenin'. I was as careful as could be. Ain't no way they saw me.'

'Jared Valeron,' Quinn disagreed firmly. 'He's supposed to be one of the best trackers or hunters in the country. He could have stood in front of a store window or something, using it as a mirror long enough to catch sight of you. I'll bet they knew exactly where you were at.'

'What now?' Eddie asked. 'We gonna let them steal our horse herd?'

'We kill them when they're stealing our horses, we've on the right side of the law. It's a whole lot better than shooting them from ambush here.'

'Did you see their numbers?' Quinn asked Porky.

'Three or four, I think. They rode through the yard, but they was just shadows in the dark.'

'That would be everyone except the one who used to carry a badge,' Stewart supposed. 'Let's get after them. If they take the main trail, we can catch them before daylight.'

'Except Porky didn't see which way they went.'

'The town of Valeron is west of here. They would have to go around the box canyon and make for the stage-line trail.'

'Grab your horses!' Stewart ordered. 'Porky, you stay here and tend the fire. One of us will return to relieve you, as soon as we run down these horse thieves.'

'Sure 'nuff, I can do that,' Porky said. 'I know how hot to keep the heat gauge. I'll watch it.'

'Make sure the catching bucket doesn't overflow,' Quinn reminded him.

'Sure 'nuff, Quinn. I'll do a good job.'

The five riders got their horses and left as quickly as they dared ride in the dark.

'There they go!' Landau whispered to Jared and Reese. 'I count five men – the three Macreedys and their two main hands.'

'I hope Shane and the Indians have a good enough lead to out-distance them,' Reese worried.

'They won't expect him to circle and head for Cheyenne,' Jared said. 'Shipping the horses by rail will not even be in the Macreedys' minds.'

'That's step one,' Landau praised the plan. 'Are we ready for step two?'

Reese grinned, though only the white of his teeth was visible in the gloom. The moon would be near full, but it hadn't put in an appearance yet. He chuckled and said: 'Let's go save a lot of Indians from hangovers and selling off everything they own – including kids and wives.'

Jared went in first, taking Porky by surprise and binding him to a tree with a length of rope. Then the three of them tore apart the still, smashed the cooking vat and busted the whiskey barrels, doubler and condenser. They ripped up the tubing and piled the rubble in the wagon. With a heap of firewood added to the mound, they shoved the burner into the mass and set the entire accumulation on fire.

There was a big enough clearing they didn't have to worry about starting a major fire, but, as a precaution, they released the prisoner and gave him a shovel.

'You watch the fire, Porky,' Jared instructed him. 'You stay right here until everything is ashes. Then you haul a few buckets of water and douse any cinders. We don't want to burn down the forest.' He stared hard at the man. 'You understand?'

'Yes, sir,' he answered meekly. 'I'll do just what you say.'

By using the whiskey that had already been brewed, the wagon had been soaked enough that it was blazing. The fire rose fifteen feet in the air, crackling and popping, its glow brightening the night, yet confined to a space of about twenty-five square feet. Soon there would be nothing left. The copper would be a useless pile of ore and the only thing left of the wagon would be axles, wheel rims and a few pieces of metal.

'You tell the Macreedys, they can report this to the sheriff if they want. We couldn't care less. This was to pay them back for killing that Mountie.'

'Yeah, I'll tell 'um,' Porky was obsequious. 'You bet. I'll tell 'um.'

Reese, Jared and Landau gathered up their horses and rode off into the darkness, heading back to Rimrock. The war had started, a war the Macreedys had no way of winning.

It was daylight before Seevy admitted there were no tracks to find.

'Where could they have gone?' Stewart wanted to know. 'They had to take this trail out of the valley. It's the only road that leads toward Valeron.'

'They didn't go this way,' Seevy was adamant. 'It's been light enough tuh see fer an hour and I ain't seen one single track.'

'Over twenty horses can't just disappear!' Quinn complained. 'Where else could they have went?'

'We kin backtrack from the canyon,' Seevy suggested, 'but them rustlers will have a full day's head start.'

'We know who did this,' Korkle pointed out. 'Let's sic the law on them.'

Stewart took the lead, turning for their ranch. 'We'll have something to eat, then I'll ride into town and file a formal complaint. If nothing else, it will get their faces on wanted posters.'

The five men set off at a good pace and reached the ranch house in a little over two hours. They were surprised to see smoke from the chimney. The surprise turned to shock when they discovered Porky was cooking his breakfast!

The five men stormed into the house as one, but Stewart was the one to speak.

'Porky! What the hell?' he shouted. 'Who's watching

the still?'

The hired man paled under the verbal attack. 'Ain't no still no more,' he muttered. 'Everything is gone. I brought in the team, but everything is dust and ashes.'

While Stewart tried not to burst a blood vein in his forehead, Porky related how three men had arrived shortly after the five of them rode off. He explained how they had destroyed the still and the wagon.

Quinn threw his hands in the air and bellowed his rage. Eddie swore a dozen different oaths, while Seevy stood with his head ducked, knowing they had been suckered. Korkle simply sat down in a mixture of despair and defeat.

'And they told you this was over?' Stewart questioned Porky.

'Yep, said this was payment for the dying Mountie they found.'

'It's over?' Eddie asked, incredulously. 'They think this settles the score?'

'They never dealt with the Macreedys before!' Quinn roared. 'We'll track them down and kill each and every one of them!'

Stewart began to pace, trying to soothe the fury that set fire to his very soul. He turned over ideas, searching his brain feverishly, trying to find a solution to the Valeron problem.

'I still say we sic the law on them,' Korkle spoke up. 'They destroyed our wagon and possessions – don't have to say it was a still. Add to that, they done stole our herd of horses. They are sure enough law-breakers.'

Stewart looked at him with a new respect. 'You're right, Korkle. We'll do more than turn loose the law on them – we'll sue for damages. We'll make them pay for the stolen horses and the wagon and stuff they destroyed. They can either cough up – say, five thousand dollars, or they will all end up in prison!'

'Now you're talking!' Quinn liked the idea. 'We'll get enough money from them to start over some place else.'

'Porky,' he turned to the hired man. 'You fix breakfast for everyone, then all of you get some sleep. I'll ride into town and speak to Donovan. I'll file a formal charge against the Valerons and we'll get the judge to issue warrants for their arrest.' He clapped his hands together enthusiastically. 'Yes! This can work out to our advantage.'

'Want me to go with you?' Seevy wanted to know.

'No, you need to get some rest. It shouldn't take me but an hour or two and I'll be back to catch a nap too.'

Reese met up with Brett for breakfast. The ladies were absent, both of them having their meal at the boarding house.

'Scarlet tells me she gave you a dressing-down,' Brett said, displaying a knowing grin. 'She can be a tiger when she gets her dander up.'

Reese felt a rush of heat warm his face and knew he was blushing like a schoolboy. 'I was going to ask Marie to come with us – I almost got it done before, but the landlady walked in and ruined the moment.'

'Speaking from experience, Reese, I never realized what I was missing until I met Desiree. She gave me a purpose in life that was bigger and better than anything I ever imagined.'

'I'm beginning to understand that,' Reese sighed, 'But,

you know, I wanted to be sure Marie felt the same about me. I didn't want her feeling beholden because we rescued her from the Macreedys.'

'She's not a kid, big brother, she's a full-grown woman. I'm guessing she is in her twenties, so she must have been courted a time or two before she was grabbed by the Indians. I'm sure she knows the difference between infatuation and love.'

'I'm not sure I do,' Reese admitted. 'I've never really had a special girl. I was always too busy running the ranch.'

'Pa did put a lot on your shoulders,' Brett allowed. 'More than he should have, actually.'

'I didn't mind. I always loved the ranch and the responsibility. Making him proud of me was all I really cared about.'

'Well, he's going to be even more proud of you when you bring that girl home. You have to know he feels he cheated you out of the girl-chasing fun the rest of us boys had. He once told me that he had pushed you too hard, that he was afraid you would miss out of the fulfillment of having a family of your own. Yep,' Brett grinned again, 'this will make his heart glad. You got my word on that.'

'How about step three?' Reese changed the subject. 'We got the horses and destroyed the still. Did you have any luck?'

'Everything is taken care of,' Brett assured him. 'You and the others best be ready. When the hot grease hits the fire, there's going to be an explosion.'

'We'll be ready.'

'I hope we don't have to. . . .'

'Oops!' Reese interrupted, while looking out the cafe's window. 'There's Macreedy.'

'I'd better get a move on,' Brett said.

'Go! I'll pay for the meal,' Reese told him. 'See you in a few minutes.'

Brett hurried out the door and went down the street. He arrived at the jail as Stewart was tying off his horse at the hitching post.

'Good morning,' Brett greeted the man, while going into the sheriff's office. He left the door ajar and took a seat behind the desk.

Stewart entered cautiously and swept the room with his eyes. A dark scowl came to his face as he stared at Brett.

'I'm Stewart Macreedy,' he introduced himself. 'Where's Donovan?'

Brett reciprocated his handle and told him the sheriff had gone to visit his kinfolk in Cheyenne. Then he added: 'As I was in town, I offered to cover for him for a few days. You know the poor guy hasn't even seen his two grandchildren yet?'

Stewart's face worked, trying to sort out what the news meant.

'You need the law for something?' Brett asked cordially. 'I still retain my authority as a US Marshal, so I can probably handle it.'

'Our herd of horses were stolen last night.'

Brett put his hands together and laced his fingers thoughtfully. 'This would be the herd of horses you stole from the Ingersol ranch over in Colorado?'

The man appeared to swallow his teeth. 'What?'

'We ran a check on the horses and discovered they were

stolen about a year ago. Ingersol wanted to thank you for holding them for him. He's delighted to get them back.'

Stewart began to sweat.

'Anything else?' Brett wanted to know.

'Some of our property was destroyed last night. I believe a couple of the men involved are related to you.'

'Yes, the moonshine operation,' Brett confirmed. 'That was on my order.'

'What?' Stewart cried.

'Brewing whiskey without a permit or paying the proper taxes is against the law. I didn't wish to arrest you for the crime . . . seeing as how you didn't sell it here in this country. But the operation was illegal all the same.'

Stewart looked like a boiler that had built up too much heat. His face flushed red, he gnashed his teeth, and his eyes bulged to hold in the increasing pressure.

'Was there something more?'

The man couldn't speak. He balled both fists and, mustering forth a tremendous force of will, managed a negative shake of his head.

'Well, then,' Brett said. 'I have one little detail to bring to your attention. Hate to compound another calamity to the night you've had, but I would like to clear it up.'

'And. What. Is. That?' Stewart ground out each word, barely able to control his rage.

'Seems the mortgage on your ranch is two months past due,' Brett said easily. 'I spoke to the banker and he is foreclosing on you. He asked that you vacate the premises by midnight tonight.'

CHAPTER TWELVE

Brett wondered how Stewart kept his hat in place with all of the steam that was blowing off the top of his head. He was about to ask if the man had any further questions when Bobby, the telegraph runner, dashed through the door.

'Here you go, Marshal!' he chirped cheerfully. 'I did like you said and gave the others to your brother.'

'Did he reward you?'

The boy's wide smile showed he had two nice rows of teeth. 'Yessir, he did – four-bits.'

Brett took the paper the youth carried in his hand and gave him another quarter. 'Job well done, young man.'

Bobby gleefully stuck the coin in his pocket and raced back out the door.

Brett glanced over the page and uttered a deep sigh. 'Stewart, did you ever have one of those days where nothing goes right? You know, when everything kind of piles up and the news gets worse and worse?'

'Never more than today!' Stewart practically snarled the words.

Brett leaned back in his chair and adroitly pulled his gun. 'You can add one more misfortune to the list, Stewart Macreedy. You're under arrest for the murder of Brock Gordon, Slick Noonan, and the selling of two Indian children while in the state of Montana. I've got a warrant signed by Judge Franklin right here.'

'*What?*' Stewart cried, his voice strained to the breaking point.

'You seem to use that word a lot, Macreedy.'

The man could hardly force out the next words. 'But. . . but this was all cleared up at the hearing for your brother!'

'Actually, no one truly believed Miss Singleton could have slipped through the shadows, cracked open a door, and put a bullet squarely through Noonan's heart. Then somehow escape before Jared could draw, turn and fire, in less than a second.' He gave his head a negative shake. 'But, we let it play out, until my sister and Miss Singleton could speak privately to the judge. They did so early this morning and he wrote out warrants for all of you but Porky.'

'There's no proof to . . .'

'Miss Singleton witnessed the selling of Indian children and she heard Seevy report the death of Brock Gordon to you. Scarlet spoke to Brock before he died and can testify as to what he said. As for Noonan, we know you killed him to shut him up, and we'll toss that in at your hearing. If you aren't found guilty, I'll see to it that you are shipped to Canada, and Miss Singleton can tell them folks how you killed two Mounties on their side of the border. Either way, you are finished.'

In an odd display of borderline delirium, Stewart threw

his hands in the air, wailed like a stuck hog, and then began to laugh hysterically. It wasn't mirth, but a release of all the pent-up steam in his system. It had to go somewhere or his head would have exploded, so it took the form of unrestrained, utterly insane laughter.

Brett rose up, moved around the desk, and removed the gun from the man's holster. Then he ushered him back to a cell. Stewart continued to laugh, hard enough the tears were streaming down his cheeks.

'I have to say, Macreedy, you are my first prisoner who ever tried to laugh himself to death, before even being sentenced to hang. Oh, and I might add, you will be sentenced to hang. Selling children into slavery and killing people is not acceptable in this country. Guess you forgot about the war we had to free all men. Well, that goes for women and children too.'

After stripping the man's gunbelt, removing his skinning knife, and checking for any hidden weapons, Brett locked the broken man in his cell.

Reese let Jared enter the yard first. He moved with stealth and was the best with a gun out of the four of them. Jared found Porky and brought him quietly out of the house. Cotton was there as a deputy and, with a little coaxing, got Porky to tell them of the sleeping arrangements.

Cotton remained with Porky, while Reese and Landau entered the house to arrest the two brothers, Quinn and Eddie. Meanwhile, Jared approached the bunkhouse.

He had his gun out and was ready when he pushed open the door. Korkle was in deep slumber, on a bunk off to his right. But Seevy had the instincts of a mountain man. He rolled out of his bed and grabbed his gun from its holster. He snaked it out and brought it to bear instantly. . . .

The gun bucked in Jared's hand. He fired twice, knowing he had hit his target, then turned the weapon to cover Korkle. He could have saved the energy.

Awakened by the gunfire, Korkle sat up in bed and paused to rub his eyes. He squinted to focus at Seevy, who had folded over his bed without getting off a shot.

'Got him, huh?' Korkle asked Jared. 'You must be pretty good.'

Jared had to smile at the man's calm demeanor. 'You're under arrest for murder and child slavery.'

He solemnly ducked his head. 'I knew I should have lit out. Soon as Eddie and the others killed those two Mounties.'

'Why didn't you?'

'Money, my friend,' he said. 'I'm too old to punch cattle or wrangle horses, and I never learned reading or writing. Stu paid me an equal share of the take. Never met a bandit or crook who would do that.'

'Guess you know the law – you were involved in the crime – so you either hang or do the time . . . behind bars.'

'I don't favor hanging, but it don't come as any surprise.'

'Put on your boots and don't try anything. I'm pretty good with a gun.'

Korkle grunted. 'I reckon Seevy is complaining 'bout your speed to the devil as we speak.'

Outside, Reese and Landau had their prisoners. Porky and Cotton were busy saddling the gang's horses and bringing them around one at a time.

'Heard a shot – or was it two?' Reese asked, cracking a grin.

'Good thing the judge didn't count on your testimony to clear me of shooting Noonan. I've seen ears of corn that hear better than you do!'

'You're too durn fast for your own good,' Landau told him. 'Proof of that is, we couldn't find a soul in town who could swear there had been two shots – and that was from two different guns!'

'Seevy was packing a .45,' Jared said. 'I reckon he's the one who shot Noonan. The man was very good at his job.'

'But you took him,' Reese praised his brother.

'Only because he had to get out of bed, before he could grab for his gun. Even then, he almost got off a shot.'

As soon as everyone had a horse – including Seevy, although he was draped over the animal's back rather than riding – Reese led the procession to Rimrock.

The courthouse was full, including people standing along the walls and at the back of the room. Judge Franklin's clerk called the room to order and the judge took over.

'Stewart, Quinn, and Ed Macreedy, you and Mr Korkle are charged with murder and selling Indians into slavery. This hearing will determine if there is need of a trial.'

'Beggin' your pardon, Your Honor,' Korkle spoke up. 'But I don't intend to make Miss Singleton sit in front of a bunch of curious spectators on my account. She has suffered enough.'

'I haven't even asked if you were guilty, Mr Korkle.'

'Shut-up! You damn fool!' Stewart demanded.

'Ah, hell, Stu,' Korkle replied indifferently. 'I ain't gonna drag this out. I ain't slept soundly since we killed them two Mounties. If I come clean, mayhaps I can clear my conscience, even if God don't chose to forgive me.'

'Take down his statement,' Franklin told the clerk. Then he looked at Korkle.

'Do you also waive the right to be defended by a lawyer?'

'Ain't no need. We're guilty of the charges.'

'Mr Macreedy,' Franklin asked Stewart. 'Do you wish to be tried separately?'

Stewart's shoulders bowed under the weight of the decision. He knew once Korkle gave his testimony they were all done for. 'Reckon we've run the rope out all the way, Judge. We'll abide by your ruling.'

It took less than a minute for Korkle to confess to the crimes. Being a master of brevity, he wasted not a single word. He ended by saying he was durned sorry for the mistakes he'd made.

Franklin regarded the four men with a grim look. 'As per the testimony, Mr Porkenridge will not be charged for any crime. Although he helped with the still, this court does not hold him accountable.' He took a deep breath and let it out slowly. 'As for you four men, the crimes you have committed are punishable by death. This court has no alternative but to order you to be hanged by the neck until you are dead.'

He looked at the carpenter. 'When will the gallows be ready?'

'I got the stuff on hand,' he answered. 'Be ready by tomorrow night.'

Franklin again addressed the four men. 'Hanging to be day after tomorrow, one hour after sun-up. I suggest you make the most of your remaining time and pray for your souls.'

He struck the gavel and announced, 'Court dismissed!'

Brett shook hands with his brothers, kissed Scarlet on the cheek, and wished Landau and Marie all the best. He had to stick around another day or two, until Donovan returned. There was a great relief to have gotten justice for the three Mounties and numerous Indian women and children. The verdict had been quick and decisive, thanks to Korkle's confession.

Reese and Marie boarded the coach to Cheyenne, while Landau and Scarlet were ready to leave via the carriage Brett had driven to Rimrock. There was waving all around and then the stage pulled out.

As Landau started his buggy moving, Jared moved over to stand next to Brett.

'Getting to be a crowd on our family gatherings,' Jared said. 'Reese and Scarlet will both be married within a short while.'

'Only leaves you and Wendy still unhitched on our side of the family.'

Jared sighed. 'I keep thinking I'll find a girl, but you know I always was the picky one in the family.'

'Your being unable to stay out of trouble might have something to do with it too.'

'I admit I've got a few flaws. Even so, I always thought I'd have a wife before you.'

Brett laughed. 'I expected to be a bachelor all my days

and yet I ended up married before Nash or even Scarlet. It's funny how life has a way of making you a part of it, even when you aren't expecting any more to happen.'

'Maybe one day,' Jared said wistfully.

'You know you don't have to stick around town. Donovan will be back in another day or two, and I'll be here for the hangings.'

'Scarlet gave her word,' he replied. 'I aim to see those four dangling in the wind before I head for home.'

'Ever hear the word "morbid"?' Brett asked him.

'Read it in a book once.' He looked at Brett. 'You calling me dark and strange because I intend to see these men hang?'

'Not exactly, but your temper and fascination with hanging people could be a reason girls aren't flocking to your door.'

Jared grinned. 'If I want advice on getting a woman, I'll ask Cliff. To hear him tell it, any woman is game for romance, if you approach them in the right way.'

'Don't go after the ones who are *game* for romance,' Brett cautioned. 'Go after the girl who wants a lifelong mate.'

'End of lesson!' Jared declared. Then he punched Brett lightly on the arm. 'Come on, I'll buy you a glass of lemonade.'